TRILETY WADE

I Won't Keep You

Short Essays & Little Fictions

First published by The Curious Word LLC 2024

Copyright © 2024 by Trilety Wade

First edition

ISBN (paperback): 979-8-9916747-1-3
ISBN (hardcover): 979-8-9916747-0-6

This book was professionally typeset on Reedsy.
Find out more at reedsy.com

Contents

Introduction

I rarely read the introductions in books, wanting to skip ahead to the chew. Forgo the foreword. And now, as I am finishing my first book, I wonder what delights I have missed all these years. So this introduction is kept short, for those of you like me who won't read it anyway.

1

Desiccation of Color and the Grey Age of Wisdom

I am the idiom for admonish. I am put in my place.

Before the meeting was casually called to order, I chatted with a City Planner who knew my Mom years ago when she chaired the county's Planning Commission. He told a tale, true to fact and true to form, of my Mom's rebuke and reprimand of him at a public meeting.

"My Mom and I have similar energies, except she leans towards provocation. She can be tough." My reply to his story was a boundary drawn between who was *"Me"* and who was *"She."*

Is every Daughter in a perpetual motion machine of see-saw slicing the umbilicus, or is it just me?

> *Tough like meat, that no one wants to eat.*
> *Not sweet like me, who will rot your teeth.*

He looked Brooks Brothers but had the alluring scent of rebel, both rare traits among city employees. As he leaned back in a chair designed for an Executive Board Room but banished to the aging restraint of City Hall, he said to me, "She had to be."

Me: "She could be tough."

He: "She had to be."

How was something so lost on me so clear to someone who hadn't seen her in decades? As if her whole life was summed up in those four words:

She. Had. To. Be.

Because she'd been. . .

Abandoned.

Abused.

Assaulted.

Yet the Planner knew none of this. He only knew she existed as a strong Woman in a World of Men.

Tough as nails that hold a home together. Not weak like me, who will yield under heat.

After the meeting, I ran into an old colleague whose appearance was unchanged: a jolly waterfall of flesh on a sturdy frame and a mess of grey curls and beard on a patient face. We embraced, and he called me "kiddo." After talking too loudly in the hallway, we went into the key-card-only labyrinth of cubicles to catch up. He told me of His Wife and their recreational pastime of feeding Raccoons who lumber onto the deck to feast on a dog food buffet.

"No shit," I said, "Mom does the same thing, and I tease her relentlessly about it!"

He's known her longer than he's known me, and his casual reply was to ask what brand of dog food she preferred. I shook my head, more amused now than critical, and explained, "She feeds them angel food cakes, pans of turkey tetrazzini, and fried rice."

"Yeah, they'll eat anything." He was unfazed by the apparent-only-to-me chasm between dog food and angel food cake. An uncrossable canyon between what is accepted and what is ridiculed. I realized at that moment how little grace I give my Mother. A grace so effortlessly given by others.

We hugged goodbye, and I commented on how glad I was that he recognized me.

"I didn't at first. You're grey now." The soft smirk of his words caressed the edges of a statement that may make another woman go mad. But it was fact, and that's how it was intended. He was an engineer through and through.

My hollow follicles give my age away, but my age has yet to give me the insight to see my Mother through the faceted eyes of a Dragonfly.

2

A Bird in the Hand is Just as Much Meat as Proverb

The endurance of backyard barbecues. Another rough rub at her patience. Wild was not allowed here, a truth verified by lawns of pristine artifice, and pubic hair trimmed to the skin. But the assumption of hair was unconfirmed because, of course, she'd never seen her neighbors naked, and come to think of it, wouldn't it be the non-wild ones who shunned their own touch only to let their lowers grow lush, or would it be the other way around where the non-wild ones tamed their hair and eschewed their own curly luxuriance?

The grill sizzled and hissed as we traded stories of our youth. I referred to myself as "wild," as I always do, and my liver winced at my spleen in a reflex of shame because all my organs knew – better than me – that promiscuity is less about rebellion and more about poor decision-making. More accurately, I was as easy as pie and as wild as a guinea pig. It's all wrong once again though, because pie is easy only to eat, but a bitch to bake. Fillings risk running loose, and crusts threaten to be tough. Pie is not a piece of cake. Even in all my guinea pig ways, I dreamed of being a curvy capybara who fucked many in a wild orgy on the shore instead of sucking one in the back lot of a bar.

I walked away from the direct smoke of coal to the slow heat of crock-pot where another neighbor stood guard over slabs of saucy pork. From the sacred vessel, I pulled out a slice of meat and placed it in the palm of my hand, lifting it to the neighbor's lips. He looked me dead in the still-living parts of my eyes and leaned into my hand to suck the sauce from the meat of pig and palm. His tongue was all muscle, and I was all nerve, as he lapped the spicy stream from the crevices of my shallow lifeline. With the tenacity of Cat, he continued to lick the pink from the pork until I was just a handful of Animal. He pressed his conspicuous chin into the fatty mantle of my hypothenar eminence, and the weight of his head reminded me I was as much longing body as longing mind. I hollowed my palm to his face so he could privately chew his secret feast in the suction cup cave of my own carving until I saw his final swallow swell his snake throat with a rodent bulge, and I wished to be a mouse. The August breeze swirled my body and whipped my drenched palm until I felt the fizzle and tingle of his saliva evaporating from my once-wet flesh.

The rest of the guests still surrounded the grill, pleased with the sacrifice to their hungry god. She was in a confused state of famished and full, and hot and cold, such that she barely registered his lips at her ear as he whispered, "If the grass is greener on the other side, then jump the fucking fence."

Originally published in the June 2024 issue of Dog Throat Journal

3

Let Me Tell You About My Day in a Dane Way

Here I am, a cadaver again. My skin the color of raw mackerel, and just as oily. So slick in fact that it's hard to hold my daughter's hand, a hand she only wants to hold when she realizes she's wounded me unintentionally. A way to soothe her guilt at causing me pain, instead of just not causing me pain in the first place. Her cooked shrimp skin is pink and buoyant, aspects I didn't even have in my youth.

I am late again. Picking her up from picking apples with the band, or was it from school? There is no clear memory in this place of present. She is critical of me, funny how you can get used to being treated like shit.

"I promise, I won't be tardy again," my exhaustion isn't because of the promise, it's just from living this death. "You know, you move a little slower when people don't treat you kindly."

My daughter stops dead in her tracks. Eyes hollow from the punch, like the black pitted surface of the moon after an asteroid attack.

7

"That's not a lesson in life," I say as I trudge away, "it's just a passing observation of my reality."

I go to find liquid friendship at the bar where the bathroom is the size of a waiting room and only one toilet sits solitary in the middle. The unattractive passive girls treat the toilet like royalty when they clean the piss of the pretty, popular ones from the cirrhosis porcelain. Opaque piss stinks, but it becomes warfare gas when you believe you're as unworthy as you are treated.

I am unobserved. My loose flesh and thin hair. Unnoticed beyond their belief that I am a troublemaker, when truly I'm a revolutionary. The piranha of pariahs, the fishiest of fin-based flyers.

My drink is as salty as my first dead best friend, whose coke-addled ghost still pours drinks for suffering patrons. Where is her picture that hung at the entrance? It's nowhere to be seen, and so I pass through the smoky sea of intentional dismissiveness, wondering why people try so hard to ignore me.

Rex sits in the rare state of being alone, brought on by the coincidence of one friend taking a piss, a second grabbing a cocktail, and a third answering a call. For one who holds court continuously, he looks vulnerable without his gelatinous protective encasement of sycophants.

"Where is the painting of Julie?" I ask him because he is the only one who may talk to me, and there's a possibility he's kinder without his entourage.

Rex rolls his eyes as only an exasperated gay man can and huffs, "It's right in front of your eyes." He waves me away with elongated Delacroix fingers of condescension.

How much effort can one man expend making other people

feel bad, I wonder as my hips hinge forward and elbows land in the wide, foretelling emptiness of the table in front of him. In a whisper of doll lungs, I let him in on a powerful secret: "I can feel it in front of me and to my side. Like how I can feel the presence of love, just adjacent to me, but I can never see it, so never receive it."

I unhinge, standing stories taller than him, "To know it's there is not enough. Maybe one day. . . " I trail off as I walk away, not caring about his faux-validating "Okay, lady" that slithered between his boulder teeth.

Not vowing to never return, just never returning.

4

My Strange Rocker

The Young misconceive the Aged, that is, until they too, become old. Harboring misbeliefs that we all evolve to be more measured in our final adulthood, a tad boring and a ton childlike. As if the wells of our passions have run as dry as they believe our tear ducts and Bartholin glands to be. We too can cry, and anyone can buy Vaseline.

I was young and blind too. Controlled by my ego, or maybe it was my subconscious, my actions originated from the deepest, unseeing parts of me. Remember the subterranean worms from the movie *Tremors*? Devoid of eyes and sight. Writhing and desirous. That was me.

I don't remember getting old.

"It's like being birthed, you don't recall it at all, but you know you're cold and exposed," was how I explained aging to a curiously big boy with skinny bones at a potluck funeral service. His eyes swelled into testicles, giving away the fact that he was now contemplating his own birth. How easily boys become Oedipal. I decided it best to prey on the appetizer table instead of the Young, so I left him to his suspension.

In my 40s, I believed it was a hoax that women become invisible with time. Figured it was just a lie told by the boring women in their latter years. Of course, society ignores you, I thought, but not because you're old, you just have less to offer, and likely always did. To think I called myself a progressive feminist when I was – more accurately – just a misogynistic ageist.

Betwixt a fuss and a rage, I finally aged as the owls followed me home not by wing but by call. Memories of men rolling their Spanish "R"s against my southern lips mix with images of Everestian orgasms, a world traveler by body if not by land. I formed eyes over the years. No longer the sightless creature that terrorized the desert, I finally saw how blind I'd been.

But now I am the sighted in the land of the blind. I am the unseen flesh. Being invisible works in my favor tho, especially as I rhythmically surge and sway on a sea of my own making. Our old porch is so offset from the sidewalk that passersby see my perpetual milkweed hair rise and fall above the wooden horizon of railing, a tuft of white silk caught in Nature's frantically aroused exhale.

Do they imagine I'm considering the next juicy, fruit pie I will bake to cool on our rundown radiator? I am. But Sundown was already personified by Lightfoot, and I am not yet Night. So beyond baking pies, I fill myself with feeling. Slide myself to pleasure.

No one sees me. They avoid the cracks in my skin and the tremors of my hands. They avoid the stoic white hair that wags from the mole on my face, like the floss tail of a tiny albino mouse tucked inside my cheek. When my pigment was still thick, I'd pluck the hair in a fit of vanity. Too simple to imagine it as the end of a little brown mouse, I saw it only as an imperfection of face.

No one looks close enough at me now to deduce the purposeful construction of the strange rocker I relax on most hours. The only joints in the frame of my hand-crafted piece of furniture are the joints in my own bones; knees, ankles, and toes. The back of the chair is my own sturdy flesh-and-bone back. The arms are my own mole-speckled arms. But instead of sitting, I kneel. My calves are cleverly attached to two curved pieces of wood, so I am able to rock back and forth of my own accord.

But the brilliance of my design comes in the pleasure aspect. Two dildos attached vertically to the back of each of my ankles. As I rock back, I am abundant. As I rock forward, I am anticipation. Candles in a perpetual pendulum of melt and remade. Or ice stalagmites in an eternity of vanish and visible. My old body hungry not for youth, but for the wise inventiveness of my double-penetrated penance for the sins I have no time to finish.

Originally published in the December 2023 issue of Dog Throat Journal

5

Conversion Vans Among Converted Prairies

Nineteen in 1994 and hemmed in by commodity crops and abandoned ammunition bunkers. How quickly quaint became barren and small became suffocating. Going from a city of 350,000 people to a town of 20,000 was more of a shock than I'd anticipated. It rivaled my surprise at the expansive flatness of it all. Those who believe the Earth is not round must have come from the planes.

One of the many jarring aspects of being human is understanding how much is forgotten in comparison to how little is remembered. If I lived in that small town for three semesters, which is around 400,000 minutes, but I only have about 90 minutes of memories, have I even lived my life at all? One memory holds on, though, with a tenacity of talons. The night I went out with the girl down the hall who came from the town with the name of Nebraska's famed red hot dogs. A foursome of me, Angie, her boyfriend, and his best friend, Mike, who I clearly recall after all these years.

The man and his van. It was red, a blend of burgundy and

candied apple. One of wine and one of carnival. A heart-shaped convex window swelled out from the inside. Before entering, you could tell he paid attention to Her, a fastidious wax and not even a fluff of dust on her surface in this field-heavy town. When the door swung open, I saw that the entire interior was covered in red shag carpet. Fat, long threads of cotton wound my fingers like the brace roots of corn, pulling me deeper into its artificial soil. But no grit or gravel was found in Her strands. He tended to her insides with the same precision as her outside, but with a suction instead of a buff.

We drove.

We drank.

We parked.

We partied so long and so far away that we stayed overnight in two rooms in a motel along the highway. Not a multistory interstate motel, but a single-story roadside motel that sleeps along the infinite rural landscape.

Mike was in the infant stages of burly and in the wise stage of tender with a gigantic laugh; a roar that rumbled the dirt roads into folds. He basked in the decadence of the mouth of my pelvis and treated my lips like an altar. Whispering his sins and kissing for forgiveness until I slow-opened to what his tongue told me. Some men lose all expression but that of intensity when in the flesh, but no matter our position or sensation, his face remained in a smile. His happiness was the pearl that I turned liquid in my oyster throat.

The next morning, I woke ahead of and next to Mike. My body was the fruit to his furry husk in front of curtains left open from the night before because there was no one to watch us but the whiskers of harvested corn. A sky of monochrome grey filled the window with the uninterested watchfulness of winter. Without a ray of sun in sight, it was hard to tell if it was 6 a.m. or 4 p.m. Either way, I knew I'd missed my classes for the day.

Still only 19, but at that moment I felt like a woman loved for a lifetime. As if decades had passed between us. . . a splendid wedding with tiered cakes and fiber optic fountains, the birth of our three boys and the hours of barbecues after games, my slow promotions and the sustainable growth of his self-owned garage, and the passionate campfires fueled by our laughter and the fumes from our bottle breath. His snoring was a soundtrack to the life I could imagine lying before me. A life where the most salient aspect was the reciprocity of loyal devotion and long embraces.

His attention and touch, I deserved it.

His kindness and respect, I deserved it.

His awe and joy, I deserved it.

Even his acceptance of the hated bits of my body, I deserved that too.

But just as always, and just like many years to come, I was terrified of being treated lovingly by a man, so his affection turned me cold. It felt safer to be trash than treasure.

I was that sky, closed off to the sun. Avoidant of warmth.

I was that field, already cropped. Nothing but stalk and knife-blade leaf.

I was that frozen air that made breathing an impossibility. The worst way to take your breath away.

Days passed, and I never picked up the ringing phone because I wouldn't have been me. I was good for one thing and one thing only, and it wasn't to be loved. And yet, we are no longer the We's we once were. But even the brightest sky and lushest field can go dark and dormant when the shame of spring's worthy warmth closes off our hearts.

6

Measure Your Success in Bat Wings

The omnipresence of bats has begun. I await the night and the wings that motor its coming. Their lateral spirals flush the day away through the Coriolis force of flapping.

Craig once said my skillet of rough-torn collard greens looked like a pile of bat wings, and now I can't cut the vegetal ribs without thinking of mammal bone and spread of skin.

I pressed my face to the screen of our bedroom window as the bats ricocheted circles in the twilight. To be so close, but so safe. Two weeks later, I woke in the middle of Night to electric sandpaper squeaks; the idiosyncratic sound of Bat. I rolled over to look at the same window I stood at weeks earlier, and clinging to the backside of our diaphanous curtains was an elongated orb of confined night.

Fuck, I thought.

A gentle nudge to Jim and a whispered, "I think there's a bat in our bedroom."

Quick as a hot dawn, we were up. One way to coax a bat from your house is to create a draft. The bat will find the wave of soft wind and fly out on its crest. So we opened a window in our bedroom and left the front door ajar to allow Jim and I to tag-team the breeze and each other. But the night was obstinate in its stillness, so the bat just flew the perimeter of our room.

Unlike owl wings, which are silent in flight, batwings emit a flutter. A vibration of air to accompany its wave of sound. And even with my head tucked under my hands, I could hear when its confusion was near. Some postures are immediately identifiable, even in silhouette, like the posture of a person making a bed or performing fellatio. I wondered if the bat could detect, with its sonar astuteness, my contour of huddling. If it could see me in a hunch, concealing myself as a nightstand instead of one who stands against night. But it ignored me as it slowed its flight only to attach itself to the wall, a miniature inverted buffalo all tucked inside itself.

So I went to the porch to be sentry to the entry of more bats as Jim tried to direct the bat downstairs and outside. I sleep pantsless in a t-shirt, like Winnie the Pooh, but even my half-nakedness couldn't relieve me from the humid heat or distract me from the anxiety of middle-of-the-night mammal removal.

But the bat was as stubborn as the breeze, so we switched places again. I added the protective elements of winter boots, a parka, and a broom to my little bear outfit and tried to shoo the bat down to Jim, who took my place at the door. After more failed attempts, we removed the screen from one of the bedroom windows and opened the upper double-hung for Jim to finally guide the silence back outside.

We ran the house, closing the openings we'd made, and tried to calm ourselves by the inspired light of the TV. Once in bed, it took me another hour to fall asleep because the energy of the bat still charged me like currents and stampedes. As Jim breathed peacefully next to me, I creased myself not into fetal, but into the efficient folds of an origami bat, trying to capture its quiet power.

After we had a second bat in our house, which occurred a few months after the first, Jim surmised I was being followed in after my evening walks, where I leave when it's light and return when it's night. So we instituted precautions that kept our home sans bats for several months.

One year later, the bats are back. They likely never left, so it's less accurate to say they are back and more accurate to say they are active. One year later, the bats are active again. Last week, as summer was exhaling into fall, I unknowingly let in another bat. Fifteen minutes after my return, I saw a shadow out of the corner of my eye in our kitchen. My first thought was that Juan had finally come to lovingly haunt me. And then my mind went rational as the bat swooped above my head, and I hollered to Jim, "Fuck!" to which he replied calmly and unannoyed, "A bat?"

"Yea, sorry," I shouted with a broom in my hand.

Within minutes, we worked together to help the bat find its way back into the outside, then Jim and I high-fived. My ice cream that waited on the counter still had its chill, and Jim's soda still had its fizz.

I wrote to a friend the other day that billiard halls are good places for first dates because you can tell a lot about a person by the way they play the game and how they win or lose. Similarly, how a couple handles a bat in their house, whether in the shock of sleep or the awareness of awake, says a lot about their relationship. We are well-lubed metal, I thought, but less like a machine and something more organic, like bone and membrane; in full flex of our couple's muscle. Before being partnered, I thought a relationship's success was based on romance alone, but maybe it's based on bats.

7

Under the Assumption of Sugar and Sweat

Misconception of culture and place preceded me on the flight to New Orleans where I acquired airplane ear in one side of my head. It took two days after landing for my stubbornly unpopped ear to depressurize and acclimate to sea level. Prior to that, my half-headedness of hearing was accompanied by a full head of tinnitus. The perceived mosquito squeal in my mind would've kept me awake in the silence of that first night if it wasn't for the February rain that fell on the rippled aluminum roof of Jeremy's shotgun house. Under an absence of insulation, the fall of water was amplified until it drowned out the tin scream in my head and became the cheapest of white noise machines.

This visit was my chance to see New Orleans before he finished law school and fled the land of sluggish sweat and seersucker suits. Jeremy's baseline behavior was "formal," a characteristic that appealed to my entirely too casual self. His formality felt contained and safe. Jeremy's baseline body was muscle, a geometric spread of shoulder above sturdy legs. I

21

wondered if his shape was a genetic inheritance or if it resulted from years of commercial fishing in Alaskan waters. His lips were usually pursed in what I interpreted as dissatisfaction with the uncontrollable nature of life. But when he smiled, his lips let up the fight and went wide until his mouth was the vast slash across an unbaked baguette.

My late-winter visit coincided with Mardi Gras, and Jeremy was eager to show me the Krewe of Muses parade, the first all-female Krewe formed in 2001. His enthusiasm was childlike and totally opposed to every other aspect of his personality. So, I readied myself for the Mardi Gras of my poorly informed imagination. I prepared for alcohol air and buoyant breasts as we left the house. But instead of boarding a bus or streetcar to head downtown, we ambled with families carrying chairs and coolers past modestly grand houses with amber-lit windows. When we arrived at our destination, I was surprised that it appeared more like a neighborhood block party than a Mardi Gras parade route. The streets were lined with ladders, all topped with securely mounted benches that were brightly painted and reminiscent of the simple open seats of county fair Ferris Wheels. Duos and trios of kids nestled into the elevated seats ready to catch beads and candy. I'd never seen ladders like that before or since, so I assume it's just one of NOLA's many baked-in ingenious traits.

The Krewe of Muses parade was gloriously orchidaceous and full of feminine power. If we hadn't been surrounded by families, I may have bared myself topless and allowed my little long boobs to swing free. But there were no tits, little alcohol, and ample room to relax, so I stayed modest. The whole evening was less raucous and more ebullient than I assumed it would be.

The next night, we headed to Café du Monde under a never-ending mist that the meteorologists refused to call rain. Beneath a tent that would usually be bustling with revelers were rows of tables only 15% occupied at best. Without waiting in line, we took our beignets and chicory coffee to the edge of the tent so we could be warmed by drink while watching the world go wet. Jeremy continuously reminded me that it was unheard of to walk into Cafe du Monde during Mardi Gras and get an immediate seat. But I remember little else from our conversation. That's the way of life and memory, the way our minds may register but fail to recall. Our lives become a picture book of feelings, like the *Pat the Bunny* book, but for adult remembering. Being a once-fat kid, tho, I always remember the food. I could've eaten an entire basket of beignets that night, but instead of gluttony, I slowed down time and ate slowly. My lips opened like a sleepy eyelid, so my tongue could see the treat and reach out to cradle the pastry, then pull it into my impatient mouth. With each press of my tongue against the sweet and greasy flesh, the beignet would deflate like cotton candy in the presence of spit. With each bite, I was satiated, but with each swallow, I was ravenous.

As we walked the French Quarter, I was constantly confronted by the iconic and ever-stunned Blue Dog of artist George Rodrigue. With a lapis lazuli coat and ripe lemon eyes, this chimeric beast greeted every visitor to New Orleans. It was in the 1990s that Rodrigue's pup gained worldwide popularity, and that ubiquity made me deem the canine from the bluebird sky - and his creator - as mediocre. My judgment made Jeremy chuckle and deem me an Elitist. For the entirety of my visit, anytime I saw the dog, I'd exaggeratedly roll my eyes as a way to belittle the tastes of the masses.

Days later, at the base of a grand and airy staircase in the New Orleans Museum of Art, I stood fully apprehended by an oil painting that was only 34 x 26 inches in size yet felt like a mural. Over 30 figures crowded the foreground in a ghostly group that stared out of the painting directly toward the viewer. All except one. The man at the head of the not-long-enough table under a generation's old oak looked away from everyone else. He stared into the parts of art that we cannot see, gifting us with a profile stoic enough for marble. Behind him was a man who leaned back on the legs of his chair to prevent being lost behind the heads of others, a valiant and successful effort to secure his place in time and oil.

The painting was more than captivating; it seduced my soul. It turned me sleepy until I woke up in its atmosphere, with that timeless group of people clothed in white who appeared made more of spirit than of flesh. I've never longed so desperately to be a part of a painting. To be drooped by the humidity under a sulfur sky. The paucity of vibrant colors coupled with the sfumato smudge blended together to create the masterpiece titled *Aioli Dinner* (1971).

It's been over a decade, and I still recall the feeling of being caught in the oak gall gaze of that painting's horseshoe group. Jeremy approached me from behind, and his presence pulled me from my phantasm fantasy. One of the most erotically charged moments of mundanity is a man standing directly behind me. Not just a random man in a queue who provides respectable space, but men I know who have subtle intentions on my body. The time the poet squeezed the space between us so tightly, I could hear the air pop like the flesh of a turgid tomato on a July vine, only to feel the seedy juice drip my thigh. Or the man who, after a night at the symphony, took me to the window on the landing of his staircase to see the moon, his body pressed behind me. He was all wood and I was all sky. I should've stayed over that night, but I was freshly sober and newly timid. Or the friend of a friend who eschewed the open gaps in a bar to tower over my smallness, less a shade tree and more the rock-hard darkness of a mountain morning, where I thrill in the potential for an avalanche. The lack of eye contact and absence of touch heightens the sensation of their nearness as their hot breath tumbles down my neck.

But this was not that sort of moment. This was simply a dear friend getting close enough to my ear to share a hilarious revelation while having respect for the silence of the museum.

With an air of justice and self-satisfaction, Jeremy whispered, "Do you know who painted that?"

"No, who?" I asked without taking my eyes off the painting.

"The Blue Dog artist."

8

The Secret of the Magician's Hat

In a basement bar with a Doberman for a doorman, I learned a life lesson. Never be the first to throw your hat in the ring of secrets.

Five of us lounged around the table. To spark the evening, we decided we'd all share one secret never before uttered to another soul. At that time, I only had a few remaining secrets, and I knew this weird group was welcoming enough to let me share with ease.

"I'll go first!"

My enthusiasm was a mix of nerves and excitement because the story I was about to tell had never been told out loud, and yet I just knew it would be a banger—one of those stories that results in an astounded pause followed by grateful and raucous laughter.

"When I was a kid, I used to poop into a magician's hat."

The story to end all stories. My opening statement would be enough to get them asking questions. But the silence was dry. Not even a gasp from their lips or blink from their eyes.

"I was just really curious about my butthole as a kid."

Nothing. The nonresponsiveness of others used to compel me to talk as if the silence between us was an indictment of my character, a badge of my boring. But silence is a manifestation of time, the tangible passing of understanding and comprehension. And sometimes silence is the fecund field of future thoughts. I knew none of this at the time tho, so I continued,

"I wanted to know what it looked like when I pooped."

Untouched drinks became aquariums for melting ice. It wasn't that my story was taking a long time, it was that no one was even drinking. Jodi just stared in my general direction but never once made eye contact. With the agility of a fly, I darted around in her cone of vision, trying to catch her attention. More details would certainly lure her, so I gave a play-by-play of my process.

"I knew I couldn't see my butthole if I pooped into the toilet, so I tried to balance on the edge of the tub and look over my shoulder to catch my reflection in the mirror above the sink. It was pretty genius, really, because the poop could fall on the tiled floor, which would be easy for me to clean. It was harder than I thought, and I just fell a lot."

This nonplussed table of cadavers was causing my mind to reel as my tongue continued to turn. I convinced myself that maybe they just didn't understand the whole story, so I kept on.

"The sliding-door closet in my room was mirrored, an excellent full-length tool for watching myself poop. Except for the carpeted floor. I considered shitting on the floor and blaming it on my stepdad's old Lhasa Apso, but I knew enough about feces to know even kid poop looks different than dog poop."

Shouldn't they be laughing? This IS hilarious, right? Even the sweetest of the group, Brett, who was always soothing of sound and accepting of thought, looked on the cusp of discomfort. His face was the polite impassivity of the uneasy half of an awkward blind date. I was the other half, oblivious. They just need more details, I thought, that's all.

"For this plan to work, I needed some sort of a poop receptacle. A bowl came to mind, but even a dishwasher shouldn't remove the shame of caked-on shit."

Have I gone too far? Was that a smirk I saw on Jeff's face? Did Elisabeth just blink or was that her subtle way of telling me to stop? No, no way, this is fucking gold, I can't stop now. My tale continued, and as the table got quieter, my gestures began to match the volume of my voice.

"So, I got into my magician's kit and pulled out the rigid black plastic hat that was too big for my head anyway. I put it on my bedroom floor - upside down, of course - and stood over it, facing away from the mirror. Then, I bent over and looked between my legs to see my tiny butthole give birth to a smooth, unbroken little poo. It was glorious!"

No roaring laughter, no eruptions of gratitude for my memorably hilarious story. The only sound was the loosening of their bodies, and the swallows as they drank deeply. In unison, they all declared that was the only secret to be told that night. I didn't ask if they took themselves out of the running because my secret was the clear winner or the glaring loser, but it was a breach of contract that I have yet to forget.

All these years later, I still stand by the glory of watching yourself shit at least once in your life. The anal sphincter really is a marvel, with its tenacious balloon-knot creases and purposeful function. A tight-lipped mouth that abhors revealing secrets, the exact opposite of the relaxed open sphincter of my old magician's hat. Wherever you are, dear Top-Hat, thank you for revealing the magic of my own body to me.

9

You're About to Hear the Butterflies Fight

"Sit soft. Sit still," the Mother whispered while arranging orange slices in her Daughter's lap. "You're about to hear the butterflies fight."

The Daughter sat cross-legged on the grass. Not the leaves of dense, plush sod you can sink into like a deep pile carpet, but the razor blades that fescue use to fight crabgrass.

A flutter of butterflies descended on the citrus buffet and expanded into a puffy storm of fungus spores. The Daughter tried to translate this unknown sound that flooded her ear canals.

Did the swarm sound like. . . .forgotten laundry savagely flapping on the line in the path of an approaching storm? Or the elliptical blinking of eyes too dry striving to self-lubricate? Or the staccato slapping of a playing card against the spoke of a bicycle wheel?

It was a sound all its own.

A flock of monarchs whose clumsy oversized wings left her little girl limbs pink with minuscule abrasions.

Incised fruit filled the open mouth of her lap with a sticky drip as the heady scent bloomed into an orange orchard in her nose. Amidst the thundercloud of flying, the Daughter's startled body became an arena for butterfly fighting.

10

The Death of a Cicada In the Garden of Life

He'd moved so many times that he stopped unpacking his books. Multiple boxes remained taped and stacked, taking up room in closets that were never big enough.

"This is why I only read books from the library now because I don't have room for any more books."

"Boxes, you mean. You don't have room for any more boxes." A cackle from her mouth cut through the cicada-hum of the garden as he turned his curious reptile neck in her direction.

"I guess that's more accurate, yes."

"Why don't you just read them, or get rid of them?" She'd had bad reactions to her constant unsolicited advice before, so her new tactic was to turn the guidance into a question.

"Because those books are just a symbol of my dead future, and I don't want to be reminded of that." His voice never wavered, never a ripple of misstep or unsure word, causing him to sound as formal as he was kind.

"Damn," she spurted, "you mean like your future dies cuz you don't read all the books you intend to?"

"No," he negated softly. "I mean, every book is a reminder of the future I didn't choose. The future of an entomologist, a naturalist. The life I could have had."

His answer astounded her into a stop on their walk. "That's a lot of meaning to put on an inanimate object."

"I guess," his response was less acceptance and more resignation.

He kept walking.

As they rounded the path into the peonies that were all leaves because it was August not May, he winced at the sound of a loud electric cry. "That cicada is being eaten."

"How can you tell?"

"Because I studied cicada calls, and that cicada is dying."

"Are you sure?" she asked while jerking her head in all directions to find the dying.

"I am 100% sure." His face was still in a flinch as if he could feel the eating. "Birds will eat cicadas the way we eat corn on the cob, with parallel chomps."

"Ugh," she was squealing and making full use of the width of the trail with her spastic hopping, "I can't handle it!"

"It's Nature." How was his doom so soothing?

Near the end of their visit, they talked about families and plans.

"You never wanted kids, right?" Her question was all curiosity and no judgment. Just a way to rebuild the Jenga tower of their friendship that had holes from all the years they went without seeing each other.

"No, I never wanted kids- - -"

"Yea, that's what I thought," she interrupted to show him she remembered the conversations from their past.

"I'm not going to condemn someone to life." His conviction wasn't tinged with passion or zealotry, just a statement of fact that being alive is a form of punishment.

She erupted into laughter, exclaiming, "God, I've missed you." And his perplexed expression made her exclamation even truer.

Growing up, she always expected the men with the most philosophical depth to be strange in appearance with an affinity towards black. But he was nearly unidentifiable in his common handsomeness: slim body, lean build, well-cut hair, knife nose, and just enough scruff to scuff during a kiss. He also never made a fuss or needed to be the center of attention with the ostentatious brooding she'd come to expect from the forlorn and dark poets of her life. Yet he was ever nightfall. Not quite night, but rarely day. More like a transition between two phases.

But he didn't know he was dark, like she didn't know she was light.

First published in the September 2024 issue of Dog Throat Journal

<h1 style="text-align:center">11</h1>

Habituating to the Absence of the Panther

W e've habituated to the absence of the panther. All it takes is time. A predator long gone from existence. Like a former lover who was fat from feasting on you but is now emaciated by your forgetfulness. They say scarcity can lead to being loved, as absence makes the heart grow fonder. But he realized that if you are not seen in the first place, then you are not missed once gone. While he'd dreamed of being a panther, he'd always felt more bat. Less speed and more flap.

Years ago, he ran away from the wife he half loved and the life he wholly abhorred. Ran away from nights he spent making love to his keyboard while she made love to the TV, neither seeing the destruction of their parallel pleasuring. That spring, he adopted a dog, not for companionship but to conceal the real reason for his evening walks, which was being away from her and being away from home. A house he didn't choose in a town that felt foreign to him. She didn't mind the canine but simply said, "It's your dog, so it's your responsibility." So he and the middle-aged adoptee ambled in the power easement, a stretch of vegetation that toupeed the buried power lines while the rest of the world went bald. The bats flew overhead, adding a click and buzz to the invisible electricity, like supplying a modern silent film with archaic audio. He nearly walked the dog to death, so chose the path of generosity and left. Not being omniscient, we don't know what happened to the pet or the wife, but we can hope they formed a bond while knowing they likely withered away in mutual loneliness.

Once he quit his life and abandoned his wife, he signed up for a life of citizen science. His earlier life as a biologist, which broke its bones into a programmer, revealed itself again, so he camped in the caves of bats, researching their deaths and disappearances. Instead of spending weekends under powerlines and avoiding the farmers market with his wife, he now spent Saturdays reading the lore attributed to the insectual crawl and rapid cyclone flight of the manus-winged mammals. He spent weeks measuring their rawbone length with the anxious tenacity he used to measure his own in puberty. How could people fear the animal that was the inspiration for DaVinci's ornithopter, with its webbed and ossified wings? With its mechanical articulation. A wonder he pondered daily. "Biomimicry at its finest," he said to fellow chiropterologists, who all nodded in unison because their respirators muffled their voices while their puffed protective equipment crinkled every conversation into static.

Even in a clan, he could quarantine himself, emotionally if not physically. Wearing identical disposable suits and masks did not make him the same when he believed his intentions to be so different. "They wear equipment to protect themselves," he muttered in the crevices of his mind matter, "but I wear it to protect the bats." He never feared other humans inhaling the virality of his escapist ennui exhales, but he feared sickening the bats. What would he do if the bats, too, flew away from the cave the way he fled from his domesticity?

"Go back," they'd bellow with the silence of their wings.

"No," he'd suffer from the safety of his cowardice.

Just another absent panther, stalking the rocky edges between lives chosen and unchosen.

12

Glaciers are the Gaolers of Floods

My official diagnosis came two years ago. But I've suffered from Cyborg Syndrome since the age of eight, when the conifers couldn't protect me from the violence of mothering. The difference between being mothered and being smothered is the difference between a wave and a hurricane.

"What if you had a mother who loved you instead of. . . suffocated you?" a question my third girlfriend asked two days before I broke up with her.

Suffocated. As if that was the minimalness of it.

Suffocated by body.

Suffocated by breasts.

Suffocated by what was called love.

If I'd attempted to answer my almost-ex honestly, I may have said, "I have no fucking clue, Amanda, but what I can tell you is that I don't date women with bra sizes bigger than A."

My snide defensiveness was the obstacle to any productive communication, even in my conversational imagination. Instead, I politely dismissed her query, "It's not really worth thinking about. Maybe curry for dinner?"

Would she have understood what I meant about my big-breasted trauma anyway? Did I even understand? I'm adept at not lying while never truly answering, better known as roundabout honesty.

The slow-melt asphyxiation that accompanies being held too long in the gelatinous fat of your mother's bosom is akin to drowning in a flood of your own tear-soaked, pungent preadolescent sweat.

I decided to go cyborg the night the needles of the pine tree compassed themselves toward me, viewing the abuse through the windowpane. The wind rustled their height, so they tip-tapped the second-story glass, trying to scrape their way in. But those needles were also tethered to the stickiness of their mother, so all they could do was be witness to the choking shame of my little-boy body reacting against my will to the caress that should have been gentle but mutated to intimate.

We are the ever unreachable.

We are the ever unreached.

And so, the panic swelled my insides; my whole body, a mouth on the wet verge of vomit.

And my fear tumesced my limbs; my appendages, cocks on the cusp of erotic compression.

"You tried," I said to the pines at celluloid dawn.

"We did," the needles yowled in the wind of morning's futility.

I spent that next morning, at the age of still 8, getting adept at self-inflicted surgery. Snipping away the smotheration of flesh and the memory of the moment I realized safety isn't for all of us. Stitching up the metaphor of meat and muscle.

Until I could remember, without sensing.

Until I could live, without feeling.

Going cyborg meant substituting data for sensation, and metal for flesh. Decades later, and not much of the original me is left.

Pines are planted to break the wind. A fortress of poke and sap. But can they attenuate the damage of a deluge?
Glaciers are the true gaolers of floods.
Potential energy vs kinetic energy.
Glaciers wait.
Glaciers gather.
Glaciers hunt.
Ever threatening to melt.

Since the night of the pine needles, 22 years past, I've gone about my days glacially. Slow and potent. I've lived my days in cyborgian security. No hurt. No despair. No embarrassment. No hate. Tho no joy. No exuberance. No excitement. No love.
Where my body was all kinetic, my heart was pure potential. How safe and contained those days felt. The ability to laugh with a disconnected lightheartedness. The ability to manipulate people into loving me from an acceptable distance. Nothing could bring me to tears, tho nothing could bring me to climax either. All rock and no release. Orgasms are an uncontrolled mess anyway - a giving over of power, like letting someone else drive. The terribleness of just the thought of it drips from my stalactite teeth, filling a choke in my throat.
Curry forged the only warmth in me, my favorite of meals. Years after Amanda and I shared our last curry, I sat alone in the Thai spot down the block from my apartment where the tiny elderly owner and I enjoyed the silently stable relationship of Restauranteur and Regular. Few words passed between us,

but she cared for me, and I was grateful. She filled my water, brought my tea, and gave me the amount of spice I needed rather than the amount I wanted.

My mostly cyborg body was still cold from the ambient winter that waited outside because metal is cold-blooded. It's strange how loneliness has a feeling, but I amputated the feeling long ago, so now I can only relate loneliness to the vague smell of mildew. Bleach, though, is a smell of cared-for. So when the aroma of chlorine crept its invisible way down the corridor, I knew the old lady had started her nightly ritual of "putting away the restaurant." Just as my tea was about to give up the last of its ghostly warmth, she came to refill me. I looked at her. My eyes vacant and mouth empty. She patted me on the hand; two appendages of time layered in a cake of vein and bone. She had poured so many teas in her lifetime that she could abandon the spout to look at me as my cup lost capacity.

"You are very American. You forget connection." Her voice was staccato and quick, like the pounding of a dozen nails in a house being built far away.

"What's that?" I asked.

"You forgot harmony. You can't amputate yourself any longer. I am your neighbor, and my house has no fence."

She removed her hand from mine and placed it solidly at the center of my back, all the while allowing me to watch her moves as if she intuitively knew about my startle reflex.

"My house has no fence," she said once again.

As the "ssss" of her fence disappeared into the steam of the tea, a rush of flood surged through my once-upon-a-time eyes, and I soaked her level chest with years of tears in the middle of the empty restaurant.

First published in the March 2024 issue of Dog Throat Journal

13

What Meteors May Come

At the age of eight, he heard the word "meteorologist" for the first time, and at that moment, his life path was decided. So he spent his weekends scouring for detritus from the sky, picking up every stone to determine whether it came from the above or the below. His identification method depended on the senses: a sniff, a gaze, a graze.

The grey ones originate in the dirt.

The ones that smelled of rain came from space.

And the smooth ones were from a source undetermined.

All his results were methodically tallied in tiny notebooks he'd thieve from the junk drawer in the kitchen. What he didn't know, and never would, was that his mother consistently restocked the drawer for him as unseen evidence of love.

By the time he was 12, he figured out that meteorology was the study of atmosphere and weather, not meteors. But he was a rigid kid and had already spent years imagining a future in which he introduced himself to others as "Andrew, the Meteorologist." Plus, the sky is the sky, no matter what falls from it.

Andrew accumulated degrees from a bachelor's to a PhD. How quickly the dunes of life amass, and yet how slowly they move across the land. Now 38, his life was a sequence of the same weather, the same mood, and the same courses being taught to students who all seemed to be taking his class as an elective. Where were the young ones interested in the ambiance of the barometer? Even the few atmospheric science majors appeared to be sleepwalking through life. Was this because their generation was doomed by the old ones who refused to retire? Or was it because, like Andrew, all these kids had also mistaken meteorology for meteoritics only to find themselves on an asteroid's altered course? While his life was now more about weather and climate than meteoroids and comets, he still occasionally marveled at falling stars.

But boring days in the classroom could crush the gut of divine desires, so he'd slump on the sofa next to the aloof cat he inherited from a neighbor and dream of being a meteoriticist. He'd wonder if kids with prominent lisps eschewed professions like meteoriticist or esthetician for easier-to-pronounce jobs like pallbearer and painter. His life's entrenched yet also somehow new-found monotony caused him to quit looking up, "Jack Horkheimer be damned," Andrew would mutter under his breath to the cat who proximally ignored him. "I've dissected currents and gasses to such a degree that the heavens no longer hold any mystery." Each haltingly haunting thought resulted in a hailstorm of aggressive caresses until the cat jumped off the couch with a hissy growl.

The next morning, Andrew prepared himself for the day's lecture. Another hour of empty-eyed students with twitchy fingers that missed their devices. He surmised that the difference between the generations was in what they held in their hands:

their phones or their genitals. He came from the latter age.

Just before the end of class, Andrew cut his lecture short to talk about temperatures. When was the last time he went off course?

"Here's a pop quiz, but I want you to vote with your hands." The silence of the hour evaporated as a few students grumbled.

"Fahrenheit or Celsius, what side are you on?" Andrew scrawled the question on the whiteboard, reveling in the absence of chalk's supernova dust.

"Let's have the Fahrenheit folks first; who's team Fahrenheit?"

The rustle of unsure students wasn't loud like thunder but loud like cinema whispers.

Of course no one raised a hand for poor Daniel Gabriel Fahrenheit and his flesh-focused method of temperature telling, because the metric indoctrination was nearly complete. But Andrew knew the genius of Fahrenheit's greater range of temperatures when it comes to the subjectivity of sensation over the objectivity of water.

$68°\ F = 20°\ C$
$69°\ F = 20.5°\ C$
$70°\ F = 21.1°\ C$
$71°\ F = 21.6667°\ C$
$72°\ F = 22.2222°\ C$

This skintuition was lost on his students, so he erased the whiteboard into a fresh snowstorm and dismissed class early.

The following week, and the topic on his syllabus – the same syllabus he'd used for eight years – was *Hydrodynamics of the Atmosphere.*

Andrew peered into the tiny sea of students, their eyes fixed on him, waiting. They had faces, but he forgot their names, or rather, he never worked at remembering them in the first place, as they'd all be gone in a few months anyway. His semester-based work schedule reflected his seasonal and cyclonic dating schedule: short-term and ever-changing.

Each student was settled in their molded plastic seats as their open laptops gave a geometric topography to the flatness of tables.

"Water has the power to quench and clean." Andrew nearly bellowed this poetic statement, but the students remained unfazed.

"Water only has power because of gravity," his voice rose again as the book he dropped from above his head descended with a thud on the desk in front of him.

"Without gravity, water loses all its power to destroy. It can no longer cut gorges. It can no longer line the pockets of roofers after hail storms. It loses the power to drown. Without gravity, we are hydrated and safe."

Glances were passed like joints between bewildered students as Andrew headed for the door, trailing this assignment behind him, "Choose carefully."

His retirement arrived before his resignation letter, and his truancy went fairly unnoticed. But the morning after a fireball streaks the sky, you can find Andrew, with his cat in a backpack, surrounded by his peers, all holding the sky's hot iron in their happy hands.

14

Stream of Heat in a Consciousness Day

I t's after 8 pm and still nearly 100 degrees Fahrenheit, yet I am on the patio watching the swallows hand Day over to Night.

My drink tries to sweat, but the humidity imprisons the drips in aluminum skin, refusing to release them. The breeze is nil, and the only artificial sound is from our neighbor's air conditioner.

Two summers ago, I read a book about the history of air conditioning and how its origin is not in keeping humans cool, but in keeping products cool. A capitalistic endeavor. Sabotaging air conditioners was the focus of one of G. Gordon Liddy's schemes to disrupt the Democratic National Convention in Miami Beach in July of 1972. Imagine the commotion and the heat. Not simply the heat of the saturated capacity of Miami's humidity, but the saturated capacity of white men wearing suits in a south coastal summer. But in June of that same year, the Watergate break-in derailed Liddy's clever AC conspiracy. And just like how David Hasselhoff's reclaimed Pay Per View fame was lost to OJ Simpson's car chase, the air conditioner's infamy was lost to Watergate.

This night heat makes my skin think it's in menopause, assaulted by one steady hot flash. But I've never had a hot flash, and I assume it's an unmistakable sensation like an orgasm; you must feel it to name it, and when you have one, you know it.

Asynchronous cicadas attempt to catch each other's rhythm, but like ill-fated lovers, their sexual tempos never align. The chorus of crickets comes from stridulation, while cicadas produce their call with the tymbal organ. A sort of accordion structure of ribs that expands and contracts in an electric click and hum. A bellow of buzzsaws. A high-decibel scratch to the itchy inner ear.

It's as hot as an eczema rash.

This unrelenting heat fries my mind and desiccates my vocabulary. I'd be fucked if you gave me a Faulkner novel to read right now. Most of my thinking was used up this morning when Doug and I drove a half-hour out of town to make our annual trip to the county fair. We've been under an excessive heat warning, so I wore a backless dress and no bra. What I lack in perk I also lack in girth, so it's only my nipples and swing that give me away. More than one kid in the parade had an intentional mullet, and we laughed at how history repeats itself, usually starting with hair.

It's hot here and everywhere. The forecast for tomorrow is a temperature of 104 degrees Fahrenheit and a humidity of 75%. Fahrenheit has a greater range than Celsius, making it the superior method for flesh-focused temperature telling. Daniel Gabriel Fahrenheit also perfected the mercury thermometer. Mercury is water's fantastical dream. I cannot hear the word mercury without thinking of Alexander Calder's quicksilver fountain in the lispy city of Barcelona. If the silvern liquid wasn't poisonous, I'd like our saliva to be made of mercury, so deep kissing would turn our chins sterling and our fevers could be diagnosed by spitting.

The air is deep and dense and makes the trees' leaves look more like they're stuck underwater than caught in the current of a breeze. A wasp floats by resembling a paraplegic hang glider whose legs got loose.

When I was 9, I woke to a fat mouth and a wasp at my lip while his swarm made a nimbus of my nightlight. I'd already been stung on the inside of my cheek when our golden retriever, Trapper, woke me with frantic barking. These weren't the paralytic wasps of summer; these were the disoriented wasps of an indoor winter.

I woke my mom and Papa John, my stepdad who was 30 years my mom's senior. He was a stocky Sicilian who owned a security company and preferred children to be seen and not heard, an agonizing task for a chatty child like me.

John woke efficiently, skipping over the transition between asleep and awake. The combination of his classic Oxford-blue boxer shorts and crisply ribbed undershirt were the vestiges of chivalric abuse and traditional masculinity. I'd only ever seen my stepdad fully clothed in his prescient Paulie Walnuts attire, so when he ran past me, I felt like I was corrupting his privacy when I couldn't stop noticing the muscular pulse of his 60-year-old quadriceps.

John rolled a newspaper into a weapon and swatted and slashed at the velocicloud of wasps as I peeked around the door at my Zorro of a stepfather. The last plan of attack was to secure the room with a closed door and a towel tucked at the threshold. That night, I slept in the guest room where the Playboy magazines were kept.

Both Trapper and I sustained multiple stings, but I can't recall the pain. I do recall, for one fleeting moment, feeling warm towards my second stepdad because he sprung into action to protect me.

It's hot like a sting. The heat that makes it hard to breathe.

15

Greasy Goals and Five-Holes

The organist slices the icy silence in a chord I can't name but is audibly and iconically the first note of the *Star-Spangled Banner*. Todd Angilly slides in with his slick of lubricious voice that lifts to boom in a matter of silky seconds, and an anthem that I have never cared about before becomes a beloved tune because of the Boston Bruins' official anthem singer. My body sways in a new looseness, all the loathing of my country's jingoistic ways melts into a puddle of humble. Todd always hits the note, never a rasp or a crack. The only miss he's made, the only shot not on goal, was when he false-started with the *Star-Spangled Banner* at the moment he was supposed to belt out *O Canada*. And just after the end of the song is caught in the net of his vocal folds, he points to fans in the crowd and makes an oscillating forearm move that is a blend of fist-pump and Guinness-pull. After each serenade, Todd tends bar in the TD Garden arena. My new appreciation for our nation's anthem and my new affection for the cherubic Angilly are just two of the many surprising side effects of my first year as a fan of hockey.

For the past seven months, my body has been under the spell of a force previously unknown to me, compelling me to stand, to shout, to wail and curse. After eighty-plus games, I am reeling and spinning, a rod and reel of overwhelmed emotion. Maybe I should've been a spectator of sport fishing instead of hockey. Maybe it's just the empathetic devastation I felt the morning after the Boston Bruins lost to the Florida Panthers in the 7th game of the 1st round of the Stanley Cup playoffs in 2023. My fanatic heart was broken. But tissue and muscle can't fracture like bone, so hearts don't break like babyface Jake DeBrusk's leg during the Winter Classic. Hearts shred, loudly, with a rip of pith and swish of skates making snow from ice. I was a heart-torn fan.

I'm not a sports fan. I'm a hockey fan.

Most other sports bore me. . . football, baseball, basketball, soccer. But hockey is my spectacle. Jim says hockey is the sport for people who don't like sports.

Hockey is my game.

I grew up around skaters, as in boards not blades. Punks. The fringe athletes. Even tho I was in high school in the early '90s, the social hierarchy of preps and punks from the '80s still spilled through the hallways, and I wasn't in the cheerleader/football fold. Yet hockey feels like the skateboarding of sports; rougher, edgier, messier. More bone. More breaks. When the puck drops, the crack and slap of sticks and ice sounds similar to the calming audio of skateboards from my youth. The soundtrack of motion and agility. The sound of freedom and takedowns. And the sound of the Misfits piped into the stadium during hockey games makes me feel even more at home with this sport.

During late spring of 2022, just before the final seven games of the Stanley Cup playoffs, Jim held the remote in his anticipatory hand and said, "I haven't watched hockey in years. Wanna watch the playoffs with me?" One hockey game in, and I was hooked. As the Avs took the cup that year, I excitedly told Jim, "Okay, I'm going to choose a team and follow them during the next hockey season!"

Never having been a fan of any team, or much of anything before, I had no idea that my naïve joy of watching two teams I had no affinity for battle it out for the Cup in 2022 would be an entirely different experience than watching a team I love be brutalized in the same battle the following season.

My scouting for a team began earnestly in the autumn of 2022 as we watched as many preseason games as possible. Which team would garner what would become my obsessive attention for the rest of the season? Like a boyfriend-hungry girl on the first week of school, I hunted the halls with the scent of blood in my nose and sniffed for the spilled oil of a rough boy in need of a soft touch.

I was thrilled by Charlie McAvoy's bruiser status.

I was impressed by the arachnid agility of Jeremy Swayman in the net.

The Bruins were it.

"The Bruins, huh? Nice pick." Jim's reaction when I told him my team. Apparently they're one of the Original Six.

Only deeper into the season would I add more meat to my roster of adoration. Brad Marchand and his aggressively idiosyncratic way of skating that Jim chalks up to Brad's short stature. Then later in the season, new players arrived. Two from the Caps, Orlov and Hathaway, and one from the Redwings, blue-eyed Bertuzzi with the flow of blade and hair, and a hockey smile that makes me jiggle like a blood clot.

Jim is from New Jersey, so he started the season with the New

York Rangers and the New Jersey Devils. The aged voice of the Rangers' announcer was a soothing nostalgia for the coast Jim left nearly a decade ago. Calling him back to his youth and roots. But when you are two people in a house with only one TV, you end up watching the shows and teams of your partner. So while Jim has endured too many hours of "Alone," "Below Deck," and sexy Spanish language shows, he was cool with watching every single Bruins game with me. Like most of our tastes, we overlap but don't totally align. So his favorite players proved to be Trent Frederick, for his assertive scrappiness, and Dimitry Orlov for his style.

Charlie, Jeremy, Brad, Tyler, Trent, and Dimitry—men who meant nothing to me a year ago—are the men we spend three nights a week with, watching their sandpaper games and esoteric crisscross of wood and carbon fiber.

My entire life has been sports-less. Barely even dipping a toe in anything close to sport or competition. But one year, when I was about 6 or 7, I was the goalie for our little soccer team. Beyond the loss of self-esteem, I barely remember anything about the experience. The other girls were quicker on their feet and stronger in their confidence. My "theory of mind" bloomed early and grew into more of a challenging neurosis than a helpful awareness, so even as a little girl, I was hyper-aware of everyone around me. Aware and compare. Faster. Prettier. Cleaner. The coach made me the goalie, and my tiny neurotic mind chalked it up to my fatness more easily filling up the goal than the other girls all lithe and light. The net was isolation and exclusion. An onslaught of ball-kicks to my face. The goalie was the target, and I was the goalie. Yet, it wasn't until watching hockey that I finally understood that the goalie is not the target; the goalie is the sentinel. The goalie protects the goal, and every other player protects the goalie.

It was during the 2022 playoffs, as I was entranced by the "big cat" moves of Vasilevskiy in the net, that I became obsessed with goalies. By October of that same year, goalie Jeremy Swayman became my favorite Bruins player. He goes from grizzly to spider in one pass of the puck. Thus, my love for the other Bruins goaltender, Linus Ullmark, wasn't far behind. And the realization hit me around the 8th game of the season; I'm a "goalie whore." Some may find the term "whore" more offensive than my favorite word "cunt," but I'm all about context and intention, and my point is, I fucking love goalies.

Jeremy and Linus are tight on the ice and even tighter off. They spend holidays together, Jeremy like an uncle to Linus' kids. I know this because a fan goes digging; a fan follows the Instagram accounts of players and searches their names for news stories. But the connection between Jeremy and Linus became a "thing" on the rink, even to the non-fans, at the start of the 2021-2022 season. After every win, the two would embrace on the ice. They'd stand opposite each other and bend over only to spring back up with blocker arms and big sticks held high, their overly-padded bodies forming X's on the ice; then they'd embrace. It became known as "The Hug" and continues to this day. For a sport full of hits and blood, this visual display of sweetness was refreshing.

Linus was awarded the Vezina Trophy at the 2023 NHL Awards. This trophy goes to the goalie considered "to be the best at this position." If you're into stats, Ullmark finished 40-6-1 with a 1.89 goals-against average and a .938 save percentage. Linus' dog died before the awards and the difficult end to the season, and he had the pup memorialized on his helmet. His eyes appeared vacant for several weeks after. The whole concept of "there-not-there" blowing a tire right in his eye. I thought about Linus' empty eyes more than my tumbling muffin of a heart can bear.

As the season continued, my hockey watching became so serious that even the phrase "activate the D," crisply enunciated by a bombshell reporter, didn't faze me. Sure, it was sexy to watch Marchand on the bench rubbing down the stick he perched vertically between his legs, all while he eagle-eyed the ice like a quick Napoleonic predator. And my eyelids quivered as I saw players stripped down to their leanness without all their layers and pads as Jim explained hockey gear to me; garters, socks, and cups. So reminiscent of women's lingerie. The tautness of straps and pressure of clasps on thighs and hips is sensually distracting, yet even the knowledge of their undergarments didn't sexualize my new sport. Hockey needs no sex to entice me.

For a new hockey fan, I was expecting a lot more fighting, but apparently the NHL has been trying to "family friendly" the sport away from its hyper-brutal days of the '80s and '90s. But what hockey does adopt is participatory violence. Players enter a contract to engage in contained aggression. Violence that won't get out of hand. I'm still confused as to the exact point when a scrum becomes a brawl, but I'm getting better at identifying when a fight on the ice is getting beyond even the referees' command. Pileups can slow-transform into writhing fights. One player checks another, or hits too hard against the glass, and suddenly each player is magnetic, pulling all the others in like steel-blade shavings until it's a black hole of bodies and a glove-littered event horizon. I am normally emotionally sensitive to yelling or aggression due to a childhood of living on the liminal shore of bruised backs and concussions. But when the violence is participatory, it becomes surprisingly emotionally calming. I am rapt at the slow-motion replays as facial expressions warp and morph, and helmets separate from heads like boosters from rockets. It's the blood that determines how bad the penalty is, but a kidney punch will get you tossed pretty quickly.

Speaking of tossing, if your salad is tossed in hockey it has less to do with your asshole and more to do with your hair. If I played hockey, I'd try and turn that into a taunt somehow, but while I'm good with word, I'm bad at insult. I take too long and cut too deep. Whereas in hockey, trash-talk has been elevated to the cerebral game of the "chirp." A chirp is inherently quick and cutting, not a howl or a yowl. Swift and sophisticated incitements get thrown like punches in a skate-by so that by the time the meaning is revealed, you're standing in an insouciant breeze of shit-talk. A chirp is often unheard, the language of the birds. Unless a player is mic'd up, you may never hear the chirp in real-time. It's the argot only of the ice, the provocative pillow talk of players.

Watching the bulk of the 82-game season was meditative. Hockey moves fast. The rubber puck, a fast-darting pupil across the white of ocular ice. My mind could settle into the meditation of movement and the collapse of time. One day, we will attend a Bruins game in person rather than watching on TV as we devour take-out Mexican. Does the crowd at an NHL game become the physical manifestation of the genius loci? The spirit of the stadium inflating our flesh with the centrifugal force of spun cotton candy. I sure hope so.

Skate blades were originally built of bone, and it's likely that the Bruins broke more records during the 2022-23 season than NHL players broke bones. But the regular season is a different beast than playoffs, an anomaly that Craig and Jim both warned me about with firm echoes of "playoff hockey is different" and "nobody is safe in the playoffs." As the run for the cup ended for the Bruins in the spring of 2023, the empathy I had for the players overwhelmed me. I turned off the TV to avoid stiff-backed Bergeron's slack face. Wanting to be ignorant of all their pain. Their sadness and second-guessing. Their disappointment or maybe rage. But Jim said not to worry, it's their job, and "they've all been there before, or will be, at some time or another."

Two days after the Bruins lost to the Panthers in 2023, Craig called to check on my mood. The year before, it never would have occurred to me that I'd need to be "checked on" because of a sports team. Before becoming a fan of hockey, I was naïve about the pull of sports. I was judgmental. Unenlightened and inexperienced. Innocent. There is an entire world behind the glass. A community of spectators and fans. Entering this world is akin to the thrill I felt when reading *The Lion, The Witch and The Wardrobe* as a kid and realizing that multiple universes can exist beyond my own myopic consciousness. The sphere of my comprehension of humanity widened, a face-off intimacy of understanding. Chalk it up to puck luck, but hockey has softened my heart, expanded my mind, and made me a part of a community.

As a lifelong Blackhawks fan, Craig ended our conversation with this instruction, "Here's what you need to remember to make the losses less bitter and the wins even sweeter; be a hockey fan first and a fan of your team second."

"But I can still fucking hate Trocheck and Gudas, right?" I spouted back.

"Oh, of course," he gleefully confirmed.

16

Photophobia's Blue Threat

My hazel eyes let in just the right amount of light, with enough bronze to block out the sky and enough green to add delight. The rays of fresh rust nestle up against the branches of pine, all enclosed in a ring of ripe olive. A confusion of color that exists in only 5% of the world's population.

Would I no longer contend with my mild body dysmorphia if I was only my eyes? Two slick spheres the color of a terrestrial starburst, instead of a corporeal accumulation of limbs and lips, belly and neck, chest and head. I'd not shrink from the gaze of others, or worry what they thought. Instead, I'd flaunt my ocular appeal. I'd pull apart the skin lids that conceal the windows of my soul to show off these oiled irises. But I am not just eye, and don't enjoy reading Bataille.

Jim's eyes are blue. Blue like his mother's and my mother's too. Blue like only one of my grandfather's eyes, as the other was hazel like mine. Blue like 10% of the world and 25% of Americans. If one-quarter of Americans have blue eyes, how did I never know those eyes can be so threatened by the light?

A few Fridays ago, when the morning was grey, and the noon hour was blue, Jim and I walked out of a grocery store into a midday parking lot. Since grocery stores are well-lit, we didn't experience the transient adaptation of leaving a matinee movie theater, with that sharp and shocking change from black to white, from dark to bright, from blind to sight. But it was still brighter than inside, or more naturally bright; the difference between the faked daylight of a Doctor's office and the reality of a sun-soaked open field.

The doors closed behind us, and we emerged from under the overhang to be completely consumed by the day. Jim's hand suddenly tore from the cart as his forearm jerked to his face. His body ricocheted back, a hockey player bouncing hard off the boards. His feet moved forward but his head kept recoiling, trying to block the light from his eyes in any number of ways, but it was never enough. The sun kept up its attack. Both hands were now on his face, so I took the cart and, calmly, aghast, asked, "What is happening?" He'd forgotten his sunglasses he told me. And at that moment, as he flailed in the contained space of his own being, I realized that I'd never seen him in the sun without his shades. His face morphed back and forth between expressions of agony and escape as if all the emotional and physical pain of his life was being funneled straight into the constriction of his pupils.

Both of us are 49, on the tremorous lip of age, waiting to be swallowed by the throaty descent of time. We are not old. We are not young. But really who can say they are only one or the other? We are all ages at once. Jim is strong, capable, and ready, but for a split second, he was Debilitation. The photophobia tore like talons. Then a sizzle and sear of heat, trying to evaporate the pools of his face. I handed him my glasses after he waved me off a couple of times because he receives help as easily as a dream receives touch, which is poorly. Once his pupils came back online and the protective but severe tears stopped producing, he put the groceries in the trunk and returned to himself.

As we drove home, Jim's purposeful blue eyes recovered, and I remembered what my friend Julie said to me the other day: "We are humans; we need each other." She has a way of pithily wrapping the truths of our lives and seeing that our profound sight comes from a sense of together instead of a state of apart.

17

The Pescetarian Paradise of Popeyes

It's been just over a year since my mom was diagnosed with colon cancer. And in a few weeks, it will have been a year since her surgery. Her hemicolectomy was originally scheduled for late April of 2023 but was moved up to April 7, the date that was known to my mom and many others as Good Friday. She was elated about the date change, saying if she died on the table then she'd be back for Easter. Her joke was nimbussed by a seriousness tho, too, as if having her surgery on Good Friday protected her; at least that's what I gathered. An omen of good fortune. My mom was raised Lutheran and converted to Catholicism but employs more of a blended sort of faith, believing not just in God but also in Gnomes, Unicorns, and Nature. The only unmixed aspect of her faith is Religion and State; she is a firm believer that religion should be separate from government. She was also a devotee of the Cult of Mary, adhering to the power of Woman as much as the power of God. I have seen my mother's face for decades but it wasn't until just now that I realized her eyes have the aquamarine hue of a pale rosemary flower, the bush turned blue by the Virgin Mary's

61

cloak.

On my mom's first night in the hospital, after our 5:00 a.m. arrival, she told me to head home at about 7:00 p.m. and instructed me to pick up dinner for Jim at Popeyes as she knew it was his new favorite fast-food joint and was located equidistance between the hospital and our home. She directed me to get a $50 bill from her backpack to pay for dinner, not because she was clueless about cost but because she's overly generous with money. I took a $20 instead, told her I'd see her in the morning, and headed to Popeyes Louisiana Kitchen.

As an aside, as opposed to other fast-food chains like Mc-Donald's or Arby's, there's no apostrophe in Popeyes because founder Al Copeland claimed he was too poor to afford the apostrophe.

As another aside, it's strange how easy it is to sound flippant when you haven't really dealt with your emotions yet. The day of my mom's surgery was difficult. Craig was undergoing a kidney biopsy at the same time Mom was in the operating room, and my negativity bias kept me thinking about all that could go wrong instead of all that could go right. I was hopped up on too much coffee from the Starbucks in the lobby, and if it wasn't for Megan in the morning and Elisabeth in the afternoon, the day would've felt like an eternity of coral cuts. Ever since Juan died, I've realized that I'm slow at processing tough emotions. Or maybe they go totally unprocessed, like the chicken who escapes the unplucking on the conveyor belt and emerges with feet still attached. I am the feathered, fearful chicken in full escape.

The drive-thru menu was an array of orange graphics, images of fried chicken, and a variety of prices. As a pescetarian, I was elated to see a fish sandwich on the menu. Jim and I feasted, he on spicy chicken and me on spicy fish, and I was hooked! Maybe it was the exhaustion from the day or the slightly lifting anxiety, but that fish sandwich was divine – crispy, pliant, and zesty.

Each flounder filet is unique, with dimensions that refuse to fit geometrical parameters. One may be not-quite rhomboid while another takes the shape of a five-sided trapezoid. Fish thicknesses vary as well, but most are bulky in the middle and taper to a crusty edge. The filets that are uniform in girth indicate a cut from the center of the fish. The showpiece of the sandwich is the slim slather of spicy sauce, the color of dried-out Dorothy Lynch. Each fish sandwich is tucked into an aluminum-lined pouch like some sort of steampunk marsupial whale baby. Jonah wouldn't have been swallowed if God wasn't so punishing. But Jonah's three-day, three-night stay in the belly of the scaleless whale gave Jesus a foreshadowing of his own dark future.

Fast food was not part of my growing up as I was raised by a mom who had very few rules, but one was about food; you must always have something green on your plate. Her other rule was that you must go outside every day. And by the time I was an early teen, she added the rule; nobody has sex in this house but me. Once I was able to drive though, I became a fast-food connoisseur. Whoppers from Burger King, a double bacon cheeseburger with a baked potato and a frosty from Wendy's, and the spinach and broccoli pizza from Sbarro; the only meal that held true to the Green Rule. By the time I turned 20, I'd been introduced to the easily chewed and impetuously fatty joys of Taco Bell. When I quit drinking six years later, after ten years of drinking too much, I quit fast food too.

Two days later, on Easter Sunday, as I was leaving the hospital, mom again gave me cash so that Jim could have a chicken sandwich. And I, I would treat my tongue to the delicacy of that New Orleans-inspired fish. But when I looked at the menu, the fish sandwich was gone, and the answer to my inquiry about its whereabouts was a crumpled intercom reply of, "The fish sandwich is just for Lent."

FUCK!

"But it's Easter," I explained as if he didn't know the day. But Lent ends before Easter. I'd missed my religious window by hours. I was both enraged at and grateful for the Believers. The rising of Christ snuffed out my fish sandwich, but the fish sandwich's existence was wholly dependent on Christ in the first place. The ouroboros logic of this seafood feedback loop left me irate and hungry.

Since then, for an entire year, I've been awaiting the resurrection of the fish sandwich. January had me scouring food news blogs and the Popeyes website. February, a Super Bowl party had me sitting next to Jason, who is an attorney and a fast-food aficionado. I inquired, "Jason, do YOU know if the fish sandwich will be back for Lent at Popeyes again this year?" My famished eyes never blinked. His laugh pounded and ricocheted the room as he looked at me intently and said, "I'm intrigued by your seriousness." I can't recall if he was intrigued about the apparent quality of the sandwich or intrigued that I was asking about fast food. For months, Jim kept patiently saying, "They'll probably offer it at Lent like last year." The day before the start of Lent, also known as Tuesday or the day before Valentine's Day or the day before Ferriss Wheel Day, I called our closest Popeyes. While it hadn't yet shown up on their website, they did indeed HAVE THE FISH! They'd had it since Monday.

At 5:30 p.m., I drove to Popeyes so we could feast while watching the Bruins' game. The line in the drive-thru was long but the lobby looked empty, so I went inside. A Door Dasher and his toddler daughter waited for an order. Bedazzled and braided, she pointed at me and began to dance. I followed suit, both of us shimmying confidently and silently. I was the snake to her charm. They left with multiple bags in hand, and now it was just me and a gal in her late 20s with fingernails several inches long that curved back in towards her hands, cradling her pocketbook. I love a woman who will eschew the heft of a purse for the handheld intimacy of an oversized wallet. She ordered and then took her place next to me by the waiting window.

The door opened, but the vestibule protected us from the wind that followed the man who walked in, looking like he'd just stepped from a New Orleans church on a Sunday morning. When I visited NOLA, I was struck by how well people wore their clothes, even the most casual dressers had an effortless formality about them. He was maybe in his late 60s, wearing a lush brown suit and a player trilby hat that capped off his sophistication and self-respect. He strode, not with arrogance but with ease, and had the essence of a Preacher. A wise orator as comfortable one-on-one as in front of a crowd. The Pocketbook gal and I both let the Preacher know that we'd already ordered.

"Ahhh, I'm in no rush," he explained.

His voice had the cadence of dark syrup and the sound of a faraway boom that coalesced into a soothing sound for all within earshot.

And then he said something about Time. . .that he looked at Time differently now, or that he didn't rush Time like he used to. . .

I can't recall his exact words, but they impressed upon me enough that I inquired, "Is that a realization that came with age, or something else?"

He put his head back as if a fly had just traversed his path too closely, swallowed, and said, "Well, you know, my wife died suddenly a few years ago."

The unresolved devastation gave his eyes a wet shine as he leaned towards us and finished, "And I realized then that every breath counts."

Every

Breath

Counts.

He gave each word its own space, sealing them in an unintentional tomb. As I left with a spicy chicken combo, a spicy fish sandwich, and two heart-shaped strawberry biscuits, the Preacher and I turned to each other. I let him know I was grateful for his sharing, and he let me know he was grateful for my Time.

I've since had a fish sandwich once a week and have two sandwiches left to go. And while other fast-food franchises offer year-round fish sandwiches, I will remain devoted to Popeyes and let six weeks of fast food be my own version of observance.

To Believers, the stylized ichthys is a symbol of Christianity. But to me, Popeyes spicy fish sandwich is a symbol of gratitude for Life and reverence for Time.

18

This Little Piggy, A Tail Told

If you find the right sinew inside a flayed fetal pig and give it a slight tug, you can animate its tendril tail. But the connection between life and death is all but lost because fetal pigs are free of blood. Their color is drab, the not-yet-pink of cooked shrimp and the never-to-be-pink of pig.

When I was nine years old, my mom went back to college part-time and graduated when I was 15. Over six years and two husbands, she earned a biology degree as a "non-traditional student." The descriptor "non-traditional" fits even her non-student status.

Little litters of could've-been-pigs populated our home for my mom's dissection homework when I was 14, and I'd show the tail trick to all my friends, especially the squeamish ones. A vase on our dining room table was replaced with a porcine fetality. The unforgettably idiosyncratic scent of formaldehyde wafted from its tray. Put winter in a cellar and make it sweat with fear, and you'll get the smell of formaldehyde. Cruel and cold.

This Little Piggy Went to Market.

67

Two blocks off Market Street, I stood alone by the window and watched the sun set on San Francisco as the wedding reception exalted in the ballroom behind me.

I was a land-locked bridesmaid in a wedding full of pilots. One approached swiftly and landed by my side at the scenery. He had Tom Cruise saunter but in a taller body. I'm a sucker for Tom Cruise in movies like *Eyes Wide Shut* and *Collateral*, but his portrayal of the balding, belly-bulging Les Grossman in *Tropic Thunder* was Cruise's most swaggering role. He commanded the scene and commanded me. I will do what I'm told 'til I don't want to do it anymore; call me the most aggravating form of submissive.

The pilot introduced himself, keeping one hand in his pocket and one in a carefully confident choke around the neck of his drink. I extended my hand, so he exasperatedly freed his, and we shook. I was taught early by my mom to shake with a firm and intentional grip, and choose the hand over a hug or a weak wave. "You can tell a lot by the way someone shakes your hand, especially a man," she'd say. What she never expressed but must have known was that her own handshake introduced her as a powerful alpha woman in a sexy beta body.

"So you're a pilot," I restated factually. Then, with genuine inquisitiveness, I continued, "Does that profession require some sort of a God complex?" His departure was undelayed. A single bridesmaid is usually a sure thing sexually, but he fucked another instead.

I am as difficult as I am easy.

How many little piggies go to market to buy, figuring out in a sizzle that they are headed to sell?

This Little Piggy Stayed Home

You don't need much to make a home except good lighting

and plants. This was never a stated design guideline growing up, yet whether with money or without, my mom chose lamps over ceiling lights and plants over throw pillows. There was never a glare, only a glow, and trails of pothos grew variegated hearts where curtains could have been. None of my friends' homes were as cozy or unique as ours.

I tried out my interior future in the diminutive reality of a dollhouse given to me for Christmas when I was 8. My mom and stepdad-at-the-time commissioned a carpenter to build me a custom-made, fully electrified dollhouse that exactly resembled our own house. The artistic license taken by the artist was a clashingly glorious hodge-podge of differently colored carpets and excessively patterned wallpapers. While the house came with a normal nuclear family, I didn't "play" house, so much as "play" designer and chef. As a food-focused fat kid, I ensured the obsolete family feasted on plastic turkeys, bread rolls imagined from individual grains of large rice, and dollops of chocolate pudding made from big chocolate chips. My interior approach to the house mimicked my childhood, with a constant rearrangement of furniture and rooms. The home held no stories of domestic romance or traditional family, because I was too busy feeding and decorating.

When little piggies leave the house, they turn from boar to pork, so they create a safety of space wherever they go and call it home.

This Little Piggy Had Roast Beef

The last red meat I ever ate fell from a man's pants. A gift in my 20s from a flirty married friend of my mom. He was one of those men who still appeared boyish even in his 50s, maybe from youthful enthusiasm or the jolly-cheeked flush of alcoholism. I would let him hug me too long and gratify him by laughing when he'd whisper forcefully in my ear, "If it's eatin', it ain't cheatin.'"

As a joke, he shoved several pounds of shrink-wrapped beef tenderloin into his jeans and gregariously pushed his pelvis toward me. I unzipped the edible gift, and the next night, 10 of us gathered at my mom's to feast on free meat, if meat is ever really free. I haven't eaten beef since.

I am no longer a non-picky omnivore rooting for worms in the dirt; I am a mouthful of my own destiny, and yet still we are hungry.

And This Little Piggy Had None

Why did the one little piggy go to the market to buy roast beef and then not share? How naïve I was to think this is a tale of shopping and sharing when maybe it's a tale of slaughter and fattening. Our plump young maturity is sent to be processed and fed to those with unsatisfied hunger.

My first fellatio at the age of 14 was with my best friend's boyfriend. He was also my first kiss and later my first sex at 16, but we never dated. We were never "public." His was the first penis I'd ever seen up close, and I incised it with my eyes; the ripples and ledges, the slit and smoothness. Whether coke or cock, if your first experience is perfect, it's easy to get hooked.

One summer night after we'd had sex, he took me with him to drive through the Taco Bell parking lot to "see who was hanging out." My face gave casual, but my insides were in a burst. The sheer joyful validation of being seen together. . . alone. . . at night. He drove slowly, because how fast can you drive with only one palm on the wheel and an elbow slicing the summer air outside? I gobbled up every single slow moment of the roll-by, wanting people to see me with him. Maybe they'd lean their heads in to say hello and smell me on his attempt at a beard. But no one noticed, and I entered a young adulthood of believing I was desired only when the doors were closed. Worthy only for being a secret. So I focused my romance on the "unavailable" of the older married poets, the religious wedded men in Buicks, and the lost espoused souls in studios. Sex was scarce, but lust, covet, and fake intimacy were pervasive enough to crush any suspecting wife's confidence and make me fear karmic retribution even years after I morally sobered up.

So afraid of being hurt, I missed that I was still the one wagging the unborn pig's tail. Trapped in a formaldehyde home all alone, I was the piggy with none.

This Little Piggy Went Wee Wee Wee All the Way Home

19

Whether Window or Door

"Heyyyy," she answered a midnight call from the number she'd known for years, drawing out the greeting until the "hey" dissolved into a smile she knew could be recognized even through the phone. Her voice was tasteful, a rich blend of silk and syrup, but also a greeting of intimate familiarity.

Most of their on-again-off-again emotional affair took place on Messenger, not the phone. But after having run into each other a few weeks ago after a spell of "off again," they'd struck back up and dove straight into phone sex. His wife was away for the weekend, and Iris was between assignations, so she was less surprised and more aroused at the unexpected call from him on the cusp of earliest morning.

Even if you'd seen him and Iris in person, you'd never pick up on their shared attraction. But as Iris said to someone's wife once, "You shouldn't be worried if you see me talking to your husband. You should be worried if you don't see me talking to him." She sauntered away leaving what she believed was a scent of mystery in her wake but was more the diesel fumes of a cheap speedboat.

One woman's perfume is another woman's choke.

"What exactly is going on between you and my husband?" Iris recognized the voice immediately, and it wasn't his voice; it was Julia's - the Wife - a woman who Iris both admired and opposed. So measured, so calm, yet underneath, Julia was the angriest of seas.

Confronted.

Iris had never been confronted before because she'd never been caught. All the other affairs evaporated before they could be found out. But this tryst spanned years, so statistically speaking, the discovery was likely. Her first emotion was alarm; her second was fear; her third was anger at him for letting his wife call her from his phone – betrayed -, and – finally – her fourth, was guilt.

Guilt is the salt of sweat and the snot of sobbing chased with the sting of acridity. The cocktail of regret.

"Uh, Julia? Um. What?" That's right, sound nonplussed, Iris told herself. Don't give her the shock she wants.

"I want to know everything. I want to know how long this has been going on. He says he told me everything, but I don't believe him." Yeah, why would you?

Finding out from the person you betrayed that your affair is found out felt like the TV dramas of her youth. All Iris needed now was a Knots Landing slap to the face and a head of feathered hair.

Iris ended the call firmly but politely, because how could she give their entire history on one phone call in the center of night?

The next day, in all her drama, Iris wanted to scratch dermatographic "A"s along her skin to build a pink chain-link fence around the house of her exposed adultery. She wanted to take charge of the chaos, everything on her terms. She would decide how news of the affair got out. She would hang herself by her own rope rather than be executed on the backyard gallows that matched the jungle gym he built for his kids between erotic messages to her.

The day after the discovery, Iris steeled herself for the fallout, believing that Julia would turn into a tell-all TV show. Selfish enough to care mainly about her own reputation and detached enough not to understand the gravity of her culpability, Iris believed betrayal could only be perpetrated by the ones who made the vows. And while she may have had her neck tied with a velvet ribbon, she never planned on binding her life to another. He was the one guilty of treachery, she was guilty only of paying attention to a man who felt ignored. Although, many men, even the ones who are doted on, feel neglected, but maybe it's more that they just aren't getting their way. The ungrown boys with grandiose erections - how she adored them.

But nothing happened publicly because Catholics like to keep their secrets.

How gullible and culpable Iris was to believe the tales he told about his wife in the first place.

"She ignores me. . . . She spends too much time mothering. . . . She thinks my interests are childish. . . . She spends too much money. . . .She prefers take-out. . . . She's nothing like you."

So Iris spent time on him. She sent him photos of buns and cakes and tits and clits. She asked about his hobbies. She regaled him with tales of her life without a family.

Wrapped up and wound up. Knowing they'd never be together but basking in being what she believed was better than his wife.

Weeks after the affair was revealed, Julia asked Iris to tea. Less to hear the mistress and more for the mistress to hear the wife. Once naughty, now haughty, Iris sat and sipped and listened. Keeping her guilt in her gut like an unbirthed fetus until it grew into a raging toddler, ripping its truthful way through her belly. You can call anxiety what you want, but it always starts in the stomach.

No longer superior and aloof, Iris met Julia on a pitch that was finally tilting in the wife's direction.

Up until this point, Iris' guilt was tempered by the fact that the affair was more emotional and anticipatory than physical, considering they'd never even kissed. The closest they came to cumming together was over cell towers. How close they came, tho, on the day he walked up to her porch with a hard-on so large she saw it through the glazing of the door. Husbands rarely walk into their own homes with a fast heartbeat and stiff flesh, but the husbands of others do, and the ability to raise the dead makes any woman feel like the most magical witch. Arousal is powerful.

It would take Iris years to realize that betrayal is betrayal. Big B or little b, it's still a bitch. Torn boundaries are like torn flesh, the best that you can hope for in the future is a varicose scar that itches you awake from the soundest sleep. But the worst you can expect is a painful disfigurement.

Decades go by, and the words of others are forgotten, but some stick. Some refuse to dissolve or digest. A rotting piece of food in the back of your throat that grows into a farm, filling your mouth with spoiled fruit and replacing your cheeks with stringy meat. That piece of knowledge that you tongue like a bad tooth. It is torturous. A reminder of how you treated people, a memento mori of who you were on your way to becoming.

The words Julia spoke to Iris over tea years ago never went away. "This didn't start when your affair began; this started when you used your words with my husband. I know you talked about sex, and intimacy, and romance. That's where it started. Your words opened a window that neither of you could close. Words are powerful, and you should treat them as such."

A window.

Why a window and not a door?

Doors open as easily as windows and are marked by the threshold of monogamy. But Julia chose the word "window," and she never chose her words lightly.

A door is for the invited.

A window is for the invading.

And so it is true, Iris snuck around under the windowsill, waiting for a scrap of husband approval as flakes of clapboard paint peeled underneath her as she crawled into a life not hers.

No Door would welcome her; she was a Woman of Windows.

Breaking.

Entering.

Thieving.

20

If One is Real, Then So Is the Other

By the time you are old, no one believes you were ever young. And trying to convince them otherwise, even with photographic evidence, is a trial at best because the structures of our faces change with age. So sure, you can share your photo albums full of dark hair, plump cheeks, short foreheads, and closely tucked ears. But as we age, our jawlines withdraw, our foreheads enlarge as our hairlines retreat, our eye sockets sink, our ears grow long with increased cartilage, and our facial fat is unevenly distributed so that we all become jowly. Of course no one can see us as we were; it is unbelievable.

Once jolly, now jowly.

Once abundant, now bony.

But he'd been old forever. Rarely remembered as young. Yet his heart was newborn even if his skin sagged with inelasticity. A jolly right ol' elf.

"Jesus and JFK had it right," he mumbled with a shake of his head as he got lost in the bathroom mirror, "they died young, so no one ever saw them old."

His wife, Beverley, heard his mutterance and replied with a

holler, "Oh Nick, stop! You're awful." Then she peeked around the bathroom door with a smirk, laughing on the cusp of her own warped joke, and continued, "Plus, you shouldn't make jokes about Kennedy."

"Ah beware, woman; otherwise, I will call ol' Yeshua. And His is a naughty list you do NOT want to be on!" They both laughed in unison, a corresponding call of pleasure, the way only couples who have been together eons can do.

She snapped his ample backside with a flour-sack tea towel that Yeshua had embroidered for her the holiday before. Bev was His favorite, and it never bothered Nick one bit. "Hey, I don't mind the attention He pays you. Women are so powerful that it only takes one good woman to be behind two great men. But can you imagine how many good men would need to be behind one great woman?" A twinkle sparked in his eye.

"Like any man would stay behind!" She clacked back with a roll of her eyes and another chap of his ass with her laser-focused snap of the towel.

It was getting closer to the big day, and they'd managed so many Christmases by now that while it was busy and bright, it was simultaneously calm and controlled at the North Pole. The reindeer were fit, the gifts were built and bundled, and the sleigh was in the hands of the best mechanic, so Nick gave everyone the rare Thursday night off. Beverley dressed up their favorite frozen pizza with kalamata olives and feta, and placed it in the middle of the table along with a stack of brittle photos.

"A salve for your ol' elderly moods." Beverly didn't explain further.

At the top of the pile was a monochromatic black-and-white photo that had been hand-colored more than a century before by a local artist from Nick's childhood village. And there he was, regal and glorious in his youth, with rosy cheeks, sky-blue eyes, and a messy mass of auburn hair. Even his suit was accurately depicted in the glossy red of candied apples and sports cars.

"Can you believe we were ever so young?" He asked his wife dreamily.

"Can you believe you used to wear this same suit in your youth?" She flicked at the fluff on her way to get drinks.

With a boisterous blast, he pronounced, "Hey, the style that made me look like a dandy back then makes me appear fucking legendary now! Nothing like red velvet and white fur."

He really did go gelatinous when he laughed, and even after all these centuries, she jiggled at the joy he emanated.

Nick ate pizza with his left hand while flipping through photos with his right, lest he get greasy the filament of memory. Images of vacations, weddings, and birthdays. Photos of friends and parties, stages and bars.

"What was that karaoke song I used to sing all the time?"

Her answer was deadpan, "Leather and Lace." After wiping sauce from her cherubic face, Bev slipped this between her sugar cube teeth, "The man in velvet and fur who wouldn't stop singing leather and lace. But Lord, how the Lesbians loved you!"

"You could've sang it with me. . . ." he winked his left eye in her direction, as all of South America went dark in a split-second eclipse.

"It is a solidly good song," Bev admitted, "and written by a woman never on the Naughty List."

At the bottom of the pile was an image of a man lean of muscle and long of height, surrounded by a group of friends of much smaller stature. The photo reminded Nick of the framed images of forgotten friendships that line the echoes of school hallways, where no one stands in isolation, and each individual morphs into a crisscross of platonic flesh that is the woven net for all of life's upcoming challenges.

Nick's eyes glistened with the shimmer of a just-licked candy cane as he whispered wistfully, "We were so young and open and wild."

Beverley looked across the table as her voice softened to chiffon, "Ah, your original Elven Entourage." But Nick was too lost in a white-out of infinite nostalgia to register her voice.

The sonorous imposition of a bottle set willfully down on the table shook him from his trance as he heard his wife say, "Well, good thing those little old fuckers are as immortal as you! Go tie one on with the boys tonight, it's still two whole weeks until Christmas."

21

Map of Nostalgia

Nostalgia's start was in a heartache for home. Yet now nostalgia is used to describe a longing for the past. I am lost and looking for a map to find my way back. If I were a Cartographer of Longing, I would chart my Homesickness for you with push pins and strings, connecting the cord between the places of your past.

A friend of mine was raised on the island of Guadeloupe. She told me of a tradition where the godparents take the newborn's umbilical cord and plant it with a tree, along with wishes and prayers for the baby to grow as strong as its sapling companion. Ray said, "In Creole, *la lombric an mwen téré,* means *home is where my umbilical is buried.*" Do Creole children suffer less from nostalgia because they know the location of their earthworm origins?

Ever a home to return to.

But, what is Death's umbilical cord? If we snip a nutrient-giving tube at birth, what bond is snipped at death? There is no regeneration of worm, only a fizzle of electric current that turns into eternal quiet.

If your umbilicus was buried where you were born in Mexico, I would tear down the tree to reach a long-ago corporeal bit of you, and I'd string it between the pins on your Nostalgia Map.

The first pin would mark the pecan orchard where your grandmother slashed "X"s in the dirt to keep the spirit-driven storms away.

Other pins would be in California, where you snuck out to see Korn or rode your bike around the high school in the valley below the bluffs where your dad accidentally shot a nail into his thigh. Or was that later in Vegas? A pin in Portland where you saw your doppelgänger, and a pin outside the convenience store where you may have seen your blood brother. A pin at the bar you tended and the prairie you guarded. Pins in the myriad people you made smile, and pins in all the people who loved you. I could pass out the pins to every soul who knew you, and they too would perforate your map with a constellation of punctures. But I hoard them like a pincushion until my porcupine body wishes for more pain to bleed the guilt away.

The last pin on your map would be on the hill in front of your home, where you opened a hole in your head for the moonlight to flood through. Telluric currents flowed from your wound to soak the soil so deeply the grass remained green long past frost.

But there are no maps, and I avoid most of the spots we used to go because of my daily desperation to make Place and Time stand still.

Nostalgically, we long for what no longer exists. But our bodies continue to recall the sensations of touch from people we love, while our minds know the truth of their absence. No amount of wandering from memory to memory will reconcile the paradox of bringing into existence that which is long gone.

Nostalgia is the word humans devised to explain away the crushing consciousness of remembering that one day we will forget all we have lost.

83

Nostalgia is the word humans devised to explain away the crushing consciousness of remembering that one day we will forget all we have lost.

22

My One Damaging Procrastination

Not one to procrastinate, I do what I should before what I want. Maybe I procrastinate living a bit, but this is about death.

I am procrastinating getting over Your Dying. I'm so slow to get about this task that I'm nowhere near the stitched seam of healing, still an open wound of ooze.

Do gunshots cauterize themselves?

Are they ragged or smooth?

You used your gun once, for the first and last time.

It was one day before the full moon when you held metal to your head. Could the moon have been Heaven dissolving the spongy darkness for you? Are you chuckling at my liberties, an atheist who now believes in Heaven because I didn't need its kindness until now?

You packed up your life and moved on, likely at the stroke of midnight. Were the owls out with their screeches and cries, trying to convince you otherwise?

I will never forgive myself for missing your suicide text. This isn't a delayed forgiveness, it's a never-meant-to-be-forgiveness.

Thus, undelayable.

I've heard that suicides are only postponed, never prevented. Yet the phrase "procrastinate my death" never made sense until now.

Did you procrastinate Your Dying?

Those moments between Drinking Tea and Emptying Your Mind?

I refuse to get over losing you. My own postponement of letting you go.

Your death is a gnarled root, extending its thirsty reach far away from the ancient tree. It trips me every time I try and soothe myself with joyful memories. Leaving me face-first in the dirt, filling my fingernails with the fluff of your ashes we buried under the mulberry.

I'm as dark as a comet's core, holding your death closer to my lava-swamp heart than I've held your life. Because I didn't see your destruction coming.

Deadlines for healing come and go, and I dilly-dally on the slope next to you in the moonlight, where the blood has washed away but the loneliness remains.

The Prairie Inhaled Your Propellant. I exhaled all Hope.

Yet you are still teaching me, from under the tree, to slow-sip the orange blossom and unlock the safe.

I promise to try and finish the task of Hurting and get about Healing.

Te quiero, buenas noches, mi mejor amigo.

23

Six Years and Two Deer Ago

After a tragedy, people say, "Something died inside me that day." Yet nothing died in me the day you died, it stayed mangled and alive. My soul has dragged itself on bloody elbows across the desert of ceaseless grief until my gooey wounds are heavy with shit and sand. Grief is like time, a nonlinear construct dressed as a sequential. It happens in a smatter, the explosion of sorrow that goes from rain to an eternal drizzle. Sometimes the drench is a quench, and sometimes the mist is acidic.

The Kübler-Ross method of grieving has been misrepresented for years. The five stages of grief were not originally designed for people grieving the death of others, it was designed for those grieving THEIR OWN dying.

Denial.

Anger.

Bargaining.

Depression.

Acceptance.

No wonder people describe their loved ones the days before

their suicides as "happy," "calm," or "content." They'd all reached the Fifth Stage of Death Acceptance.

You endured the five stages of grief without me. I am caught again in the barbed wire. How many times did you release me? How many pairs of my pants required mending?

There are no stages of grief for the ones Left Alive. Our sorrow is cyclical. We grieve like the phases of the moon, from sea-foam light to obsidian night.

The fifth anniversary of your death felt worse than the first because I was getting used to you being gone. But after trudging the attritious road of worn down until I was devoid of bone, I decided that day to hike the forest we always trekked together. The bur oaks were still as gnarled. The hills still as steep. The aggressive red of sumac and the delicate blue of aster still told of Fall without a calendar. I feared I'd be flooded with memories of you, overwhelmed in a torrent of remembered forgetting. But instead, I was buoyed by memories of others too, and I realized that I'd been tending more to my grief than to my loved ones still living. My body lifted to the liberated lightness of bird bone and powdered down. I was on the verge of flight for the first time since you died and I finally felt you by my side.

Each anniversary of your death brings about a new mood, though, and by the sixth anniversary, I was polar and opposed to the fifth. Grief and guilt are the froth and fault of suicide's habitual whirlpool, and I am the eddy your parents warned you about as you stepped into the river of your independence. My mood was pure Growl, and all I could think about was how you ravaged your skull to release your mind but I was not around because my phone was set to "Do Not Disturb," and you likely believed that you were my Disturbance.

You are not the Hole; You are the Heart.

I am the Bullet and the Take Away.

But you were my Spirit, the bifold of my Soul.

Years ago, we sat at the window in your bedroom and watched the deer yearlings that I called "unspotted fawns." You removed the screen so I could photograph them without obstruction. I didn't ask. I never had to ask. You just knew what people needed. Like the time I had a craving for dark chocolate in the middle of the night and you rolled over and pulled a bar from your nightstand. Or every time you sensed a shift in my mood, and smoothed whatever stippled me. So we sat, silent in our watching, as the two deer who entered the woods behind your house separately, came together closely. Both feeding at the base of the same tree, their necks and heads in parallel so that their bodies resembled their own cloven hoofs. Cleaved yet cleaving to one another. Until one raised its inquisitive head and walked away. We were the deer; separate, bound, separate again. One deer stayed, and one walked away. Neither deer was just you or just me. But I miss chewing grass with you by the tree.

24

Safety of Inimical Wheels

You won't register its presence by sound, at least not at night. In fact, if you depend only on sonics to know when it's at your back, it'll be too late. It's the light that gives it away. A violent light that quick-carves the cone from your retinas, removing all color perception so you forget the brilliance of blood but remember the monstrosity of serrated-bladed pine trees. You have only two ways to see now, scorched or sharp shadow.

"Shadow at night?" you wonder.

"Moon and fire," you remember.

But stop debating with yourself.

Can't you feel it coming?

It hurtles towards you, screaming around curves of once-upon-rock, a beam of light erupts in a reach from an unfastened mouth; the arm will catch you. All darkness is gone in the blink of your burning eye as the beast spotlights all that it's about to devour. The spotlight of surgeries and raids. Only the shadows will keep you safe. Wait until it passes by. The predatory machine that skips time. Eating its own history, an ouroboros of slowly digested technology. How do you still exist? A fossil just as fast as the past, leaving severed limbs in its path.

This is trickery.

You are being lied to.

I'm not telling you about monsters.

I'm telling you about tracks.

The trains.

With their roaring ferocity.

The way they rush you like an orgasm.

Or leave you in a tempest as they pass.

And how they eradicate night.

If you've never lived near the alley of loud tracks, then you aren't intimate with the rails' scream; not high like migrating gulls, and not wet like slaughtered lambs, but more cold, like metal dentures grinding together under the weight of a nightmare.

My safest sleep has been in houses next to tracks. Both day and night, trains made their way along the hips of a river. While the daytime trains blew their horns to satisfy your frantic wanting waves, the nighttime trains would squeal and quake.

The trains' reflective echo of loosened boulders and squirming steel will subtle-nudge you with each pass until you feel the protection of a lion set loose at the end of your bed to gnash your bad dreams away. You may have thought that your guardian angels don't travel, but they send the trains to crash through the darkness to shield you when you are away from home.

25

The Misunderstood Beach and Its Mnemonic Emesis

The sea's belly is regurgitated seasonally, and this is what we call a beach.

A never-ending tidal turnover of sand and memory. Sand isn't defined by its material, but instead by its size. So if the grain is small enough, sand can be anything from quartz and cliff to lava and fish shit. Beaches aren't always sand tho, sometimes I'm told they're cobble.

And yet we lay our bodies in the detritus and exfoliate our toes, trying to bury ourselves in its physics. It's a place of joy and remembrance. I think. Though I'm not really sure as I'm a child of landlock. My experience of beaches by the sea is limited to two, California and Florida.

In California, I'm told by my mother that the beach was my toddler-realm more than the water. And I remain liminal to this day.

In Florida, I walked through the mangroves on an April morning to reach the beach as the air turned grey. The entire stretch of sand was without people; it was just me. And then, in the expanse under a sky that refused to rise, there was a sole windsurfer. He was defiant in his miniature verticality, and I wondered if he thought the same about me. I had never felt as connected to another human being as I did in that moment. But that was when a thick distance was what I needed to feel anything.

At our family's cabin, the lake's beach used to extend uninterrupted from water to door until a seawall was installed; a formidable 3-foot-tall wall of wood that amputated the shore from the wave. When I was a kid, too fat to feel at ease in a bathing suit, I'd skip rocks instead of swim or ski. Searching for the debris of boulders with fingers and toes is a calming practice broken only by the repetitive splash of the stones' ongoing conflict with the water. Stone skimming was a pastime that brought me and my dad together with nothing more needed than a shared goal in parallel. We'd hand congratulatory nods back and forth until the lakebed ran out of rocks. To this day, he's one of the best skippers, a trait of fatherhood if not always fathering.

During lake days, as everyone else drank and lounged on floaties, Juan would spend hours erecting rock structures along the seawall. His half-submerged body was a watery centaur erupting from the cove. By the time the grill turned on, the wall was crenelated by his cairns. The same wall that separated the lake from the land became a shelf of Juan's showpieces. Dad still shows me stones he pulls from the lakebed, which he believes originated from Juan's sculptures. Instead of coveting the gems, we put them back on the wall as a way to stop the slough of time and marvel at the past that the lake gives back in an act of mnemonic emesis.

26

Cinematic Intimacy

The cinematic intimacy of couples on screen gives us a chance to see into the lives of others without being peepers in real life. So instead of watching couples on trains or through kitchen windows, we can lean into the screen and become an invisible third in a party of two.

John & Holly

John McClane landed in L.A. an hour ago to visit his estranged wife on the night of her company's Christmas party in the Nakatomi Plaza. He sponge-bathes the airport off his body in Holly's private office bathroom as she casually chats and occasionally fidgets. It's been a while since they've shared space, and now they commune in that quintessential marital expanse of the bathroom. For never having been in her office before he seems at home, more because of her presence and less because of the carpet crushed therapeutically between his toes. Their conversation is cozy, and warming its way towards John staying at her house instead of with an old buddy over an hour away.

And then, like any hopeful conversation can do, this one takes a tumble. In the lobby below, John just found out his wife has been using her maiden name, Genarro, instead of her married name, McClane. He was hurt. He was stunned. A fist to the gut by a loved one who didn't even know they threw the first punch. Feelings of rejection and abandonment coalesced quietly into a resentful and angry grenade in his chest. But Holly doesn't even know the missile exists, so she heaves a sigh of vulnerability and says, "I missed you." John lets silence fill the room with its flammability before saying, in an I've-got-you tone, "I guess you didn't miss my name tho, did you?"

The rest of the short scene is the archetypal relationship argument characterized by interruptions and raised voices. Holly is trying to be emotionally unbuttoned, but her voice goes scorpion as John continues to be insouciant with his words. In refusing to meet her openness with his own, he opts instead to grab the whip from the metaphorical wall and implode the moment so she will know his pain without him having to speak it. Each lash from each tongue generates a new wound, and if it hadn't been for the greedy Gruber, Holly would likely still be a Gennaro and John would've spent Christmas in Pamona.

Die Hard, 1988 – directed by John McTiernan

Mary & George

Mary has been trying for months to be noticed by George, but he's too distracted by his lifetime of sacrifice to see her, so she sets the mood with moon music to awaken his memories of one forgotten night together. But he's still stick-hitting the picket fence in his mind and delaying his entry into the parlor of her life. A call from Sam Wainwright severs the awkwardness, and Mary immediately turns on the charm for the man with an offer of ephemeral affection for her and ground-floor plastics for George.

George and Mary share a phone because it's the 1940s, and there's only one phone per floor, if that, so their heads nestle into a similar space as he steals inhales of her hair without her noticing. Mere inches apart, their Rubin faces create Rubin's vases as Mary whispers intensely and breathily, "He says it's the chance of a lifetime." George throws down the phone, torn asunder by his conflicting desires, his love for Mary and his lust for a life outside Bedford Falls.

He shakes her hard by the shoulders and shouts, "Now you listen to me, I don't want any plastics, and I don't want any ground floors, and I don't want to get married ever to anyone, you understand that?" His bellows may be aimed at her face, but he's yelling at himself. Then George finally embraces Mary, squeezing her head in his hands as he realizes his true feelings that burst like a climax. But instead of drenching her cheeks in semen, he covers them in kisses that crash land like the airplanes he will never fly, choosing her as his sky. This tenderly aggressive scene is all face; it's porn the 1940s way.

It's a Wonderful Life, 1946 – directed by Frank Capra

Bill & Alice

Alice is in her underwear, consisting of a less-than-opaque white camisole and panties. It's as simple as it is sexy. Slightly girlish but also womanly. She is in an intimate conversation with her husband, Bill, who is exasperated and tired. Mid-argument, he arrogantly clarifies his take on the situation, "You got a little stoned tonight, you've been trying to pick a fight with me and now you're TRYING to make me jealous." But Alice isn't trying to make him jealous so much as trying to be seen for the fullness of who she is.

Earlier in the night, when she donned a second skin of velvet and lace, her eyes in a faraway gaze, Bill said she looked great without even looking. So now, stoned and worried he had sex with two models at the holiday party, Alice tells him a story of a naval officer on a while-ago family vacation; "He glanced at me as he walked past, just a glance, nothing more." But that glance was momentous. Just a pass of a stranger's eyes over her body elicited a fantasy in her mind where she left her husband and daughter, just to be desired, even for one night. All as a way to explain to Bill that it's not just men who struggle with hunger; women also want the eerie glow of blue deceit that washes the invisibility from our limbs.

Like Holly and John, Alice and Bill are separated by space. She coils into herself as he sits rigid in a posture of attack at the edge of the bed. They are far away from each other, unlike George and Mary who were in the proximity of touch.

Alice explains from her spot on the floor, "At that moment my love for you was both tender and sad." She is not sobbing, she is not performative, she is simply exhaling her carbon dioxide words to make room for the oxygen she longs to breathe. The sheer honesty of her love, as she tells him how she "thinks" about her love for him, is what makes this scene as revolutionary as it is awkward. But the true exquisiteness comes in Kubrick's deft reminder of how artificial we can appear even in front of the person who knows us best when we don't feel known at all.

Eyes Wide Shut, 1999 – directed by Stanley Kubrick

Lorna & Martin

Lorna and Martin are examining their scars in a warm

but bureaucratically furnished Spanish colonial home in L.A. The investigation starts at her wrist and continues along her forearm. He untucks his shirt to show her the shag carpet remains of being dragged half a mile by a moving truck down Ventura Avenue. She unbuttons her Henley and corrals her mane to expose an old bullet hole through her shoulder. He illuminates her skin with the desk lamp under which she just stitched him up. A new wound behind his ear, a graze of the skull, now sewn tight like a zipper. The inventory of injuries continues along his back and at the base of her rib cage until he's bare-chested and her shirt is untucked, but both of their belts remain buckled.

In an excited effort to share the healed wound on his right thigh, Martin begins a swift unbuckling. The clear click and clack of the unclasping is unforgettable in its enthusiasm, like a kid at *Show & Tell*, full of delight and easy confidence. But Lorna's mood flips on a nickel, and she turns away immediately, sensing the sheer sexual power of a belt being undone. She side-eyes the loosened leather like a serpent dead-set on penetration and continues her quick gait of walk-away.

She's done.

He's clueless.

He pushes the rolling office chair out of the way with his leg because his hands are still in full grasp of the snake at his waist. Lorna has the statuesque expression of a woman pissed, with a clenched jaw, tight corner lip, and eyes that settle into a sharp shape of judgment. The storm of her agitation formed so fast that Martin is unaware of the drench.

His pants are down to his knees so he's covered only by black briefs and boots. Seconds ago, there was no distance between them, and now the physical gap is a canyon expanse. He's looking at her; she's looking away, saying only, "I'll take your word for it," as a polite but firm way to say, "Put your pants back on."

Once she catches his gaze, his eyes go soft for just a moment before they go hard again as he says "Hey, you started this." She retorts with a quick clip of "Yeah, well, I can end it," as she tears her headband from her head to let her hair conceal her profile and curtain the anger of his stare. She enters his space once more and they fuck on the floor anyway, but an unbuckled belt can be buckled again and a woman can say no to a man. No matter your gender or your lover, remember Lorna's words and that you are in charge of your ending.

Lethal Weapon 3, 1992 – Directed by Richard Donner

27

When We Are the Progenitors of Our Own Pain

The Wee One preferred fields to sidewalks because the former held no cracks. No gaping gullets between slabs of concrete emerging thirsty for rain and broken bone.

Sidewalk travels required her ocular attention, whereas running the meadow held no fear of snapping her mother's spine.

Step on a crack, and you'll break your mother's back.

This threatening rhyme became possible fact.

Hops, skips, and tip-toes over every split in the road were her attempts at control because trauma breeds a need for sovereignty.

"Why can't we just walk on the sidewalk?" Her companions would whine.

"What's wrong with taking the long way around? There are raspberries along the backs of lawns, but just grass along the sidewalk." She was influential, not from coolness or skilled oration, but from certainty. No one else at the age of 10 had enough assurance to disagree, so they'd all walk the circuitous path of patchworked yards instead of the steadiness of cured cement. And she breathed easier for it.

At the slight age of toddler, she witnessed the beating of her mother, who'd witnessed the beating of her mother, who'd witnessed the beating of her mother. Genetically disposed to Man's violence.

Horizontal hail of fists to face.

Thunder stomps of boot to back.

The metallic snap of bone is buffered by the muffle of flesh, so it's more of a thud than a shatter. But the Wee One swore not to snap her mother's moon skeleton just to get to school. She could not bear being the perpetrator of more punishment.

If bone is made of moonlight, is the moon made of bone?

The Wee One grew, as did her superstitions. Concrete-crack-skipping turned into wood-knocking and earlobe-pulling, which mutated into compulsive counting and obsessive organizing. The only relationship she could ever commit to was one of ritualism.

Now in her 30s, the Wee One's friends were less apt to follow than her 10-year-old compatriots. Her crumbling turned to avalanching, so she started to strangle her superstition with science. Petri dishes took the place of dinner plates. Bacterium took the place of pets. Her nervous energy found a focus in research—anything to keep her mother's bones whole.

It took more than several months but less than several years for her to develop a bacteria-based self-healing concrete. With each spine-threatening crack that appeared, her bacteria were there to catalyze the invasion of oxygen and water, and convert the nutrients to limestone. From fractures and fissures to fixed and firm, the process repeated itself again and again and again

- a reliable restoration – until all the sidewalks were whole and urban living became liberating. The sidewalks, trembling with various shades of lung-colored gum, basked in the Once-wee One's not-yet-insouciant stride.

Her fear of being the progenitor of her mother's physical agony should have evaporated now that the world was devoid of concrete cleaves. But her ache wasn't remedied.

The fear of flesh, torn and saucy. The fear of hair, uprooted like weeds. The fear of eyes, timid with betrayal.

It was all still extant. For while concrete could now heal itself, she could not.

One day, far in the future, the Wee One will find herself scaling a mountain where Nature thrills in mars and flaws, and stone relishes in its wrinkling. The crevices will feel the softening of her tentative soles. Her steps will fill in the cleft's emptiness as a lifetime of alarm is finally silenced. Her footfall will have no effect on her mother. No hammer to glass. No door jamb to skull.

She will be set free. A life of open ladders, fearless mirrors, and Friday the 13th soirees.

But for now, she stands stuck in a meadow waiting for rain because even the earth has betrayed her with its drought as the thirsty clay separates itself into claw marks and cracks.

28

Hobbled By Subtle Lies

We are undeniably gorgeous when we allow ourselves to be loved.

The people who know me best would say I have a bit of body dysmorphia, a smidge of body issue. But it's more a terror of being witnessed unedited; uncropped and filterless.

The fear of being "seen" in all my nudity has obstacled me in the past. Your body won't open to touch if you're too focused on concealing your dense folds of Shar Pei belly skin. And you can't let your limbs be free and ecstatic if you're attempting to dam the delta of flesh that spreads from your arms and chest.

Somewhere in my rearing, I believed I would be judged wholly, solely, mostly on my body.

Was it the way the 3rd-grade boys cackled when Mrs. Pitt wore a sleeveless blouse on a hot day, teasing her that she could fly away with her wings of pendulous flesh?

Was it because one grandmother got drunk at a family dinner when I was 18 and affirmed with a clink of her martini, "Trilety, I love you. But you're fat!" Our family argot includes her oft-said facts about life: "You can never be too rich, too thin, or have too much storage." It's hard to disagree with the storage one!

Or was it because the other grandma convinced my mom to enroll me in a weight loss program when I was 15 because my legs had a "good shape," but you know. . .I was "heavy." This grandma was a bombshell brunette beauty in the '40s, but she shorn her hair after my grandfather's affairs and battled her body for years.

My grandmothers were not the progenitors of the propaganda so much as the victims of it. They were the victims of the Madonna Whore complex, where men were taught to want wives who could offer Doris Day's girl-next-door dedication in the kitchen and Marilyn Monroe's sex-kitten energy in the bedroom. And the daughters of our grandmothers were the victims of the models of impossible Barbie dolls.

We are all perpetrators and victims at one time or another, as I have caught myself judging others as much as being judged. But mostly, I watch other women with amazement, in awe at how their storm-cloud cellulite doesn't prevent them from being loved, and how they don't see a need to apologize for the space they take up, whether physically or intellectually.

During a recent visit from my dad, we mirrored each other's crossed-arm stance in the kitchen and talked about the family reunion I missed.

"I only knew the people in your generation and older, and most of those people are all passed," was my explanation for my absence.

"Hey kid," he cocks his head, arms still crossed, "I get it."

And he does get it. And he gets me, even tho I can be bewildering. My dad and I don't go deep, but we go wide, like the river he lives by.

He shared stories of the reunion, of the sweltering heat and the food. And he told me of his cousin's wife, describing her as "a knockout, a real Looker."

This is not a slight to me, but I compare anyway. Because being a "knockout" with my dad's approval was my goal growing up as a dorky, fat kid.

"And she can drive equipment too, and work with tools." He continues to praise a woman probably my age or just a little bit older. And I continue to compare myself to her, even tho none of what he says has anything to do with me. Because I can barely get the roll of packing tape on the packing tape gun without Jim's assistance, let alone command a truck or crane.

"My cousin, though, he has the family curse," my dad says as his face wrinkles like someone in the path of halitosis.

"What's that?" I ask, not recalling ever hearing about a curse.

"You know, we have a tendency to be portly or rotund," he explains with a bit of blowfish breath to his cheeks.

I laugh. He laughs. We laugh.

Both my dad and I are formerly fat, but he seems to approach the world of overweight the way former smokers approach cigarettes, with a compassionate disgust. In all honestly, I do the same. Maybe it's because being confronted by an abundance of weight strikes me with fear, not of my own past corpulence but a terror of how unjustifiably unworthy I felt when fat. My admiration was immeasurable for women who were unashamed about their bodies, who strode through life wearing their value like a designer dress. I dressed down, to match my esteem. Maybe my dad is the same, fearing the man he was before the loss.

Lately, I've been watching the Netflix show "Queer Eye: Germany," the same country where I eyed my first penis as

I swam in a hotel pool and emerged to a naked couple also taking a dip. The woman left no recollection in my brain, but I could build that man back from my memory alone if you gave me enough clay and a skill for sculpting.

There is a moment in every Queer Eye episode where the "star" of the reality program shows off their new style of hair, makeup, and apparel. In the 2nd episode of the 1st season of Queer Eye Germany, Ulli struts into the living room where not just the Queer Eye crew awaits her new look, but her husband too.

Uli's body shape and weight are unchanged because the Queer Eye crew stays only a week, with just enough time to transform the home and a wardrobe. The denim of her jeans clings in a desperate desire for her lusciously plump thighs, and her hair, now out of the daily constraints of a ponytail, has a bit of lilt it didn't have just a few days before.

But the real change is in Uli's energy and attitude. It is this transformation of the way she sees herself that stuns her husband. Our eyes are the giveaways of our truths and lies, and his eyes gleam. On the verge of cry, he utters "I'm speechless."

The physical transformation of Ulli is barely there, mild at best, but what her husband witnesses again for the first time in so long is a woman who sees what he has always seen; worth and beauty.

Jim sees me like this, unconcealed in my Ulliness. We can spend a weekend together doing chores and yard work, unshowered, my hair an oily tempest and my comfy clothes hiding any sense of hip or tit, and he will wink at me as I walk by, his blue eyes crystalline and say, "I love you!"

Victims of propaganda don't know they've been victimized. And it's tough to even identify the propaganda that results in us believing a lie. But by the time I am more wrinkle and crease than supple and silk, I will surely be 100% de-propagandized. Until then I will try and exist in a natural state without the voices in my head telling me to cover up, to be ashamed, to stay away. I will unleash my never-ever perky breasts and let my dress linger on the ripples of my flesh. I will attempt to care more about who I am than how I look, and remind myself that this body will dry out and degrade, so I should live in the flesh I was given. Easier said than done, but I will try to just loosen the fuck up.

29

Proving Him Wrong is Proving You Like Him

"Why do you think Jesus is portrayed as sexy?"

She rolled over onto her elbow and propped her head in her hand awaiting his attention.

Andre stayed supine staring at the sky and picking at a piece of grass instead of his abused cuticle.

His answer was nonchalant, with an air of *I don't care* or *I've thought of this before, so already have the answer.*

"It's probably that whole young-death-apotheosis thing like Cobain and Kennedy."

"Oh yea, definitely," she agreed, all the while making a mental note to look up the word a-paw-thee-oh-sis.

"Do YOU think Jesus is sexy or do you just think everyone else thinks Jesus is sexy? Because those are two different issues entirely."

Conversing with him felt pedantic and clinical, and in 10 years' time, she'd tire of it and treat their lingering friendship like a succulent you're gifted on Administrative Professionals' Day. But today, she was still in the State of Enamor.

"Well, I mean, he's never been MY type," [*both Authentic and Western Jesus looked nothing like the man she was trying to impress*] "but he's always been presented in a sexy way. Hair on the verge of drying, curls buoyant like breasts, and all those elongated fingers on the cusp of caress."

While her words came naturally, she was still intentional about trying to seduce with verbiage. She figured if her physicality wasn't a lure, then maybe her mind was. But she didn't even know the word apotheosis so suddenly her head felt as fat as her body.

"But that's not necessarily the way others present him so much as it's the way YOU perceive him. You are the one sexualizing Jesus, not the artists."

Matter of fact. He was a legal document that delivered paper cuts along with obfuscation so you were both confused and in pain.

She hated how Andre believed he KNEW her, but her only emotional equipment at the time was a patient pout. It was easier to let him think he knew her, because she barely even knew herself.

Later that night, she obsessively scoured the internet and her old art history books for evidence to prove that Jesus was sexy beyond her own imagination. Skipping dinner and forgetting to feed her cat, she congealed all the corroboration into a gouty document that she typed up, ready to hand deliver to him at the next night's dinner.

She could tell that he could care less about her findings as he skimmed the document for holes in her argument. But what she couldn't tell, as his pasta lost its heat, was that he did care. He cared that she spent all that time trying to prove him wrong; she spent all that time on HIM. His pride and cock swelled at the thought of being someone's Sun. . . of having a Satellite. For years, he maintained his gravitational pull on her, keeping her moored of her own accord, in the tiny orbit he let her have.

But only the Hindsight Lion knows that with enough time, Jesus would've been a bald man with a pot belly, and she'd be a woman who didn't give her time to a man like Andre.

30

Nothing Unbearable Lasts Forever, Even Yourself

She stole his hand from his pocket in an absconsion of palm and went to whisk him away, introducing herself in a hurry, "I'm Milan, like the author."

But her name was really Camilla. And she already knew him as her partner.

Camilla renamed herself as Milan because she'd just finished *The Unbearable Lightness of Being.* The book, not the movie, as Camilla claimed to commit herself to the purity of word and refused to see any book-to-film adaptations. So, with the flick of a name change, she wrote her own new narrative and detached her retina reality from her fantasy eye in an attempt to go blind.

Little did Camilla know that her favorite secret movie was based on a book. Thorp's novel *Nothing Lasts Forever* became the movie *Die Hard,* and so Thorp's Joe Leland became McTiernan's John McClane. When others would talk about action movies, Camilla would wave her hand to shoo away the swarm of invisible flies and their trail of bad taste while saying,

110

"I prefer Jodorowsky and Švankmajer to any American-made action movie." She had a clear idea of the person she wanted to be all the while ignoring the person she was. It was lost on her that liking Jodorowsky and McTiernan were not mutually exclusive, or that people with "taste" were not much fun.

In her post-Kundera haze, Camilla felt dizzy and dazzling in her search to find power in her weakness. She wanted to wreck the boredom of her relationship with drama and agony. So she tried to run away from this mundane Sunday by pulling her boyfriend into a romantic gallop, hands wet with sweat, hearts connected in the arc of a tragic romance. But he slipped his hand from hers, looking both bewildered and annoyed, and huffed, "Enough games, Camilla. Let's just get brunch. The line is down 20 people by now." She responded with a whisper, "It's Milan." Though she hated brunch, she was hungry and out of ideas.

As he read Baudelaire on the balcony choking down the only scotch he could afford, she secretly listened to Celine Dion in her headphones. But when he asked what she was listening to, less for the sake of curiosity and more because he enjoyed being either generous or stingy with approval, she lied and said, "I'm learning French so I can finally read Molière in his native language." His eyes gave just a hint of sparkle as he nodded and returned to his book. Camilla had no intention of reading Molière, but she'd heard his name in a matinee showing of the classic movie from her parent's generation, *The Breakfast Club*.

When you spend 100% of your time in a relationship being hyper-aware of trying to please someone, it's likely less of a romance and more of an illness. Or it will make you ill in the end. High alert is what she would've called it had she had more self-knowledge, but in the obfuscation of infatuation, she just called it caring.

It was tender to be attentive to every one of his expressions and gestures.

It was nurturing to notice whether her behavior changed his mood.

It was simply observant to be keen-eyed to which women surrounded him and who made him smile the widest.

Being with him meant not being herself, but being Milan was a betrayal as well. A sly and subtle way to show him that who she was, was not who he knew, because she'd learned early in a family of judgment to conceal her true self. Milan was liberation and choice. Camilla was sway and stay. But Milan was made up and Camilla was substance.

Years later, Camilla will find out that *Die Hard* is based on a book, and she will buy it immediately before boarding a train to Lithuania. *Nothing Lasts Forever* is much darker and way less sexy than its movie adaptation. Joe Leland was 25 years John's senior and was visiting his daughter, not his estranged wife. The terrorists included women who were just as wicked as the men, and Joe's daughter goes tumbling backward out the window along with Hans. There is no heroic salvation, only lonely heroism. The only other character left alive besides Joe was Sergeant Powell. It was a genuine buddy cop book, but capitulating alcoholism and tragic family histories were stand-ins for comical one-liners and love interests. She read it in one sitting and realized she now had two loves, the movie and the book. Camilla closed the paperback and thought back to that day waiting for overpriced eggs in the Eastlake neighborhood of Seattle and realized she'd misread Kundera and should've grabbed her own hand, not his, and broke loose that day.

31

The Power of the Her Hyena

Long too little, I sought to be powerful. So I found a model of feminine in the female spotted hyena, who gives birth via clitoral delivery, through an elongated stretch of nearly eight inches of flesh. This is twice the length of the innervated wishbone clitoris that lies hidden in human women. My clitoris is like the rest of me, diminutive but longing to be prominent.

When a female hyena is full of birth and belly, she will endure a transfiguring delivery. Down comes the cub through the clitoral birth canal to erupt at the tip with a rip like the burst of a hot dog that is deep-fried until its oil-soaked insides explode and shred the ends into ragged cut-off pork shorts. It will take weeks for the mother to heal, leaving her clitoris topographically scarred forever.

Beyond birth, the hyena's clitoris is also used for urination and mating. Urinating through the clit didn't shock me because I thought mine was the same organ as my urethra until my 20s. The propinquity of the tip of the mountain and the start of the sea.

But the sex is astonishing. What is the process of mating between male and female hyenas, each equipped with two tubes of flesh? Will one tunnel of muscle enter the other tunnel of muscle in an extreme version of "urethral sounding?" If "urethral sounding" could get any more extreme. Or maybe it's more like a man falling in love with a butterfly and learning the anguished ecstasy of the proboscis penetrating the narrow regions of his penis.

To measure the depths of the sea with antennae. Would you choose to be the deep or the feel?

If you read further into hyena research, at some point, you will come across the phrase, "It is possible for female hyenas to achieve erections." Ah, the concept of an erection as an achievement. . . who knew getting hard was such a feat? But even human females exercise the specialized skill of achieving erections, we just aren't as bombastic about it as the males. With the female hyena as a model, I would long less for a cock and more for the coil of a serpentine clitoris that could rest in my lap when apathetic and strike with a lengthy lunge when erect.

Female hyenas become erect to show submission in the presence of a dominant female.

Astounding.

What if an erection in the human world signified submission? Not dominance.

What if the slack flaccidity of a male symbolized power? Not weakness.

The sophistication of a loose penis is underestimated. The relaxed phallus appears calm and knowledgeable, a dick that will listen and offer you a cognac. Whereas the authority of an erect penis is inflated. It can be less five-star General and more like a demanding child, desperate for attention. Society undervalues the charm of a well-boiled slippery noodle over the ossified crack of rigidly raw spaghetti.

Female hyenas are aggressive and dominant. They do not flaunt so much as stalk. I am as passive and submissive as I am bold and dogged. I need the power of the hyena in me. To flash my button of flesh as if it hung a hand's length between my thighs, one inch thick in the middle and ruggedly exotic from trauma. We grew up being given the model of a hard man to understand strength when we should have iconized the clitoris of hyenas instead. Let us tear off our underwear, spread our lips and stick out the tongues of our cunts to wildly expose our proud potency for pleasure and capacity for pain.

32

Decomposing a Fantasy

*H*ow many of our sexual fantasies are resigned to the cutting room floor of our imagination? And how many of our erotic daydreams are better dreamt than done? Her thoughts wandered in the grocery queue as she sized up the size of people's produce. She knew better than most that living is often duller than fantasizing and that the hurricane of hope can be downgraded to a boring storm where the most you'll get is a soak.

If two exes ago hadn't finally let her lick his eyeball, it would surely still be in her rotation of self-pleasuring images. The sensation was memorable, more cohesive than Jello and firmer than aspic but with a panna-cotta surface. His eyeball accepted her tongue with just a bit of give before the membrane repelled. The feel of his tongue on her eye was akin to fine grit sandpaper, and she felt accosted by a needy cat. What she thought would be a thrill was more like an empirical science class.

While she'd never touched herself to the idea of sitting on citrus, she got slick sitting on an orange for hours in nothing but a slip at the command of a long-distance lover. But her knees soon climaxed into cramps, and arousal quickly fizzled into tedium. The scent of citrus on her labia was the one plus to that experiment.

Reality is Fantasy's mundanity.

Back at home, in the cardigan reserved only for the eyes of her cat and with a cup of tea in her hand that she drank between coffees as her minimum attempt at living healthily, she flipped through the old National Geographic magazines that came with her eccentric inheritance.

Beyond the bareness, it was the vultures that caught her eye. The May 1968 issue, which was mostly devoted to Finland, had a spread on vultures and their tool-using abilities to crack eggs. She didn't know how many dozens of eggs she'd wasted, let alone how many dozen she had left inside her, but the idea of yolk and choke stimulated her thinking. The author's early words let her know that the vulture was a bird she could relate to, *"At first we saw only a confusion of vultures gathered round about 20 ostrich eggs, squabbling over the contents of some that were broken."* To be confused and argumentative were two states she understood intimately. As the author went on to explain the vultures' carrion ways, the descriptions made her body tense with want and thought.

Before the article was finished, she was flying into a fantasy of "vulturing," where one plays dead, and the other plays the bird. She imagined herself fully clothed and supine with an unknown lover dressed in feathers and squat-walking around her faux-dead body.

Hovering.

Observing.

I am new meat to your beak. I am your shock and flee. The poetry in her mind accompanied a pulse in her pelvis.

You lack a voice box, as vultures do, so you hiss and gasp and grunt. I lack a pulse, as those newly not of this earth do, so I lie lustless in a hump.

Would she leave her eyes open or conceal them under a rigid lid? How else could the dead beg to be plucked by tongue and talon if not with the expression of pupil dilation?

A brush of broad feather on my breast. A clutch of long claw at my thigh. How deep inside my body will you dive your bald head? Feasting on my emptiness as my insides slip from your featherless scalp, keeping you clean for the next quench.

In reality's harsh light, would she even be able to stay still under the keen investigation of a lover dressed as a vulture? Or would she be distracted by the jiggle of her belly awaiting the drench of his frozen oil feathers? But roleplaying as the scavenged dead would be the perfect scenario to avoid nudity, to stay clothed while they stayed plumed. Nakedness isn't needed in this game; just the feel of a fake, hooked beak confidently tearing the barrier of her skirt would bring her to shiver. In the flesh and in the fantasy, her body was consumed in a flush.

But what partner, or partners if she was considering a flock of fucking, would participate? Who would understand this was less about sex and more about the vulnerability of staying prey. Accepting the risk of torn heart and scratched skin.

Conceding to be seen.

Swelling to be smelled.

Yearning to be learned.

The ease at which this dream could be replicated in real life electrified her limbs in ecstasy, but then she wondered if it would fall flat in the way of pupils and fruit. Is this just another sensual invention she keeps for her own self-pleasure? Because as she orgasms at the thought of her carcass being consumed, she knows she is just the skittish wind tempting the noses of those sniffing for fresh flesh. But vultures don't break the morning like robins; they mend the day through salvation. And she will run away in anticipatience as night dawns and morning comes to detect her on the breath of birds.

33

Elbow Bend and Back Again

Knowing his desire for eyeball-licking, she was ever on high alert for women whose eyes bulged above their cheekbones like fresh breasts. Just once, two years ago, she gave in to him and allowed the nubby rough of his tongue to press into the gelatinous give of her eye. Distracted by the possibility of pink eye tho, she never let him lick again. She shunned the eyeball the way most women shun the butt.

During their recent movie night, she picked Bull Durham because she remembered her mother loving it. Her mother, the last in a long line of Barbaras, broke from tradition and named her daughter Barbie instead. So Barbie and her beau settled in for the late 1980s movie and watched as Susan Sarandon slipped on screen as waifish of limb as she was whisper of voice.

But Jesus Christ, her eyes. Annie Savoy's thyroid eyes popped off the screen with glisten and thirst, and Barbie's PVC heart raced in panicked jealousy of a woman now her grandmother's age. Barbie squirmed in the crease of cushions, fidgety of finger and mind, until her boyfriend laid a calming hand on her thigh as the other hand casually tossed popped corn into his mouth.

With timid inquisition, Barbie muttered, "Wow, those are some big eyes, huh?" desperately begging him to validate her normal-sized seeing.

"Ha, I guess anything looks big on a woman that small!" He cracked himself up so much he missed her getting smaller beside him.

"God, does he think I'm fat?" she thought to herself, just another pummel of self-abuse. Just another insecure incision.

Ken found Barbie beautiful. But he told his best friend that it felt pointless to tell Barbie that when she'd just object.

"Sounds like you feel unheard, man." His best friend shook his commiserative head.

"Yea, I guess that's it. Or, ... I don't know, I guess it feels like she thinks I'm lying?" Barbie's boyfriend avoided eye contact, not wanting the depth of his sadness to be seen by his best friend.

"That's rough, man." Another understanding head nod.

"Yea it is, thanks, man."

"Man." That was the word they substituted for the act of hugging. Two rigidly limbed men born of hard plastic fathers and raised in homes where hugging wasn't just not allowed, it was physically impossible. How do you hug without joints?

Beyond Barbie's jealousy of eyes was her jealousy of elbows. So many other women - especially the women more worldly than her - had pivot points in their arms that allowed for a bend where she barely had a bow. Ninety degrees of confidence in a sleeveless dress.

Women with hinged or permanently bent elbows could put both hands on their hips in a stance of power and erect breasts. Whereas Barbie's arms were either straight at her sides or straight above her head, no other leeway was allowed to her noncompliant limbs. She'd sit beside her boyfriend and side-eye his Instagram feed as he scrolled mindlessly on weekend afternoons. Images of women with elbows in the crow yoga pose atop mountains barraged her from his phone until her insides turned yellow celluloid: the plastic of the old dolls. The color of the left behind.

Her mood would go sour and pout. He could feel it, the drifting away. When her acetate hair went flotsam on the waves of her stormy mind. Little did Barbie know that the importance she thought he placed on elbows was all her own projection. Ken adored Barbie's never-bent arms, especially the arm's length hand-jobs and the way she went Frankenstein when in a run.

Barbie felt most cozy when alone with her beau at home. But every other weekend, they played in a local kickball league. A gathering of 20-somethings in personalized jerseys drinking beer and playing baseball with an inflated rubber ball - the sport of childhood. Those days were tough for Barbie. Most of the other women were athletic, with names like "Swim & Dive Barbie," "Flippin Fun Gymnast Barbie," and the most deadly, "Karate Barbie."

Emblazoned across Barbie's jersey was her moniker, "My First Barbie." Nothing sporty about her or her name. Even worse, the other women were bendy of elbow and had a high-five habit that kept their joints smoothly lubricated. Barbie didn't know if she could high-five because she only tried it once in 3rd grade. Her fully raised arm overshot the other child, and she fell into the air, a clumsy missed connection for all to see. She could still hear the cries from the playground that day as she ran away, "Straight-armed Barbie can't high five!" High-five anxiety dogged her til this very day.

If Saturday afternoons were spent at the kickball field, then Saturday nights were spent with Barbie in a mood of sullen avoidance as her beau felt helpless to save her. He'd reach across the couch to caress her knee and stare at her with tender, questioning eyes. He was trying to let Barbie know he loved her. Wanting to ask why she refused to let him do so. But all Barbie saw in his vulnerable sight was pity. He couldn't possibly love someone like her. How could he ever love someone so insecure, so incapable of putting her hands on her hips in a sassy manner? He must be biding his time until "Karate Barbie" broke up with "Karate Ken."

They say that gaslighting is done to us by others but sometimes we are the ones who gaslight ourselves until we've warped our own reality so badly that there is nothing left to question and no one left to love.

You are the ever-observant sibling of your older sister's self-induced catastrophes. Barbie is blind to herself, living in a land of shameful make-believe. But you, you're Chelsea, you are the Virginia Slims doll for the 21st century. Your durably blue-shadowed eyes are illuminated by the sizzle of a No Vacancy sign. You are fully occupied.

"Call me Chrysanthemum," you demanded of every teacher until you were 12. Never afraid to change your name or alter your ways. How did you get so bold? Where some girls had older sisters who were bossy, you had an older sister squishy with self-doubt, so you became the muscle, and she was left to be the thin skin. Hairless skin was one of the rare sister-similarities you shared. In high school biology class, you'd laugh and compare yourself to a pig gone fetal, as Barbie chewed her pen to oblivion and scoured the arms of the other girls to compare hairlessness.

And when it comes to men, you've never been afraid of their coming and just as unafraid of their going. They're not the food you eat to survive, they are the food you eat to get happily fat. When you were 13, the boy down the street brought over a small duffel he called a "doctor's bag." If you'd ever opened it, you would've found it stuffed with the saccharine innocence of Twinkies and Nerf balls.

"Face the wall," you said to him. Was this the moment you realized you took after your favorite but estranged aunt, "Kissing Barbie?"

Ricky did as he was told, and you pressed your impossible breasts into his back and corralled his chest with your ninety-degree elbow bend. If his neck had any hairs, they would've stood on end at the graze of your nose behind his ear. And when you whispered, "Are you ready to melt?" he matured to frozen petroleum.

With the rest of the family home, you kept your clothes on, but directed him to do as he was told. How many hours did you make him sit at your feet only to let him pat your ass just before the dinner bell rang? You didn't know that your older sister was watching, ever unblinking, in awe of your command and his obedient need.

Your existence made Barbie feel even more unworthy. How naturally you cascade through life. How powerfully you throw your head back and laugh, cracking open skies and raucous gatherings with your carefree cachinnation.

Friends approach you at parties with some variation of, "I knew you were here the minute I walked in because I could hear that laugh of yours."

"I laugh like I orgasm," you say, "intensely and spontaneously!"

There are women with better jobs, more lovers, longer hair, but you are too busy living to notice, let alone compare. That occurred to you a few days after your older sister asked, "How are you never jealous of anyone? You're just so at ease."

"Jealousy is resin," you declared with a swish of your hand.

"Yes," cried Barbie, not sure what you meant. "God, I'm jealous of that."

You and Barbie cackled and giggled in unison at the hilarity of her dramatic irony.

"Hey, let's go to the park. I want to practice something with you."

The next three hours were spent in high-five attempts. Barbie's sword arm would slice the sky as you'd direct her to back up a bit, explaining, "Your arms are longer and more rigid than others, so you'll have to judge the distance just right."

Barbie wanted to be molded into other women, but you were showing her that molds are made to be broken. This is why you chose to teach her this lesson in a public park instead of your private living room, so that she could *become* in front of others. Fall and get back up. Be witnessed, and not care. Passersby would linger a little and you'd wave them off, directing Barbie to pay attention to the moment at hand.

Over and over again, she'd fall into your goalpost arms, and you'd catch her. Minutes before the sun set and the air was still amber, your sibling hands finally made contact with a muted clack that rang like wedding bells, and you embraced as best you could, two sisters finally on equal footing.

You can't teach someone to love themselves, but you can teach them to high-five, which is a solid first step toward worthiness.

34

Belle Isola

Only the big toe knows that flip-flops were designed to isolate. The strap that separates the big toe from the rest results in a particular sort of loneliness; to be so alone, yet so close. Belle's contemplation of her sandals did not weigh on her buoyant innocence. At this age, she was simply noticing, not yet at the age to project and burden the world with meaning.

Between the peaks of 5 and 7 is the age of 6, the cusp year between awareness only of self and the later awareness of others. Belle was 6 and on her first of many summer trips to Hilton Head Island with the whole of her family. Siblings, parents, grandparents. Belle had spent an hour standing in the Atlantic as waves rushed her ankles. She felt a rebel immersed in water while still wearing shoes. Almost as adventurous as her older sister, but less so because Belle didn't want to drench her dress. The spray from the Sea's roaring lisp soaked her anyway, without full submersion, so all was okay.

Belle proceeded to ponder the pink plastic cleave that turned five individual toes into two divided groups. It was a split she could feel. A cut the color of tongue that sawed incessantly against her vulnerable skin. Even when she stood still, the toe-post made itself known, needy for the attention of flesh. She'd think back to that memory, while in heels or huaraches, and wonder why she hadn't tossed the shoes into the ocean.

"What were you thinking out there?" her grandmother queried, beer in hand and toes shoved in the sand as Belle made her way back from the water.

"About my wings," said Belle.

Her grandmother shook the condensed confusion from her forehead and waited patiently for an explanation.

"My shadow and my reflection, they make wings," Belle explained while wringing out the hem of her wet dress.

The mother of Belle's mother cocked her head back as if she'd been slapped and pulled her phone from her beach bag to see the photo she'd earlier snapped. And there it was, Belle's shadow and Belle's reflection radiating from opposite sides of her body, the incorporeal wings of her little bird being.

Belle's observation stung her grandmother, who normally loved the ocean because, in its roughness, it refused to throw back clear reflections, unlike the quarries she used to skinny dip in when she was a teen. But Belle was right. There was a reflection, it was just folded like a paper fan.

There is no escaping yourself, thought Belle's grandmother, so you're never truly alone.

"What are you thinking, Grandma?"

"Oh, I was just thinking about how isolation is a context, but loneliness. . ." she exhaled, "now loneliness is a feeling."

Belle's wet dress snapped and flapped in the ocean wind like a flag around a pole.

"Do you remember when Barbie said she didn't have a vagina,

Grandma?

Belle's hysterical but muffled giggle from the movie theater two days earlier returned, but now she howled with a liberated larynx.

"That was funny!" she yelped,"Barbie is funny like you." Off Belle flew, now without her second wing, just a long shadow that told of Night's coming.

After the family was full on corn and crab, Belle's grandmother walked down to the beach. Vacationing light saturated the sky, but not enough to dissolve the spilled-salt of stars. She walked into the water, sandals still on, and looked up into the night. The sea frothed at her feet, and she felt each burst of ocean bubble against her sensitive flesh, imagining each foamy wave was the rippling gas of faraway stars fizzing into twinkles. Waves of light and waves of water, the oscillation of celestial ocean and effervescent sky trying desperately to meet each other.

Belle's grandmother wished she could photograph herself in this moment, the way she photographed her granddaughter earlier in the day as a reference photo for one of her oil paintings. To see herself from a fathom. Not as far off as a star and not as close as a kiss. To paint herself in impasto at the edge of this island. She even chose a title, *Isola*, the Italian word for Island, and a proximal root of the word isolation. At that, she cackled, for everyone knows that choosing a title for a painting that isn't painted is a sure way to kill the project.

The night was not done, and she was not tired. So instead of heading back to the rental, she stripped herself of her dress, kicked off her sandals, and said to the sea, "I AM as funny as Barbie, and just as old," and with that, she dove under the crenellation of wave and swam until morning.

About the Author

Trilety Wade writes essays, little fictions, and poetry. The *body* is a running theme in her work, and while she's a rule-follower in life, she sometimes shuns rules on the page.

You can connect with me on:
🌐 https://thecuriousword.com